D0149699

What the press says about Harlequin Romances...

"...clean, wholesome fiction...always with an upbeat, happy ending."
—*San Francisco Chronicle*

"...a work of art."
—*The Globe & Mail*, Toronto

"Nothing quite like it has happened since *Gone With the Wind...*"
—*Los Angeles Times*

"...among the top ten..."
—*International Herald-Tribune*, Paris

"Women have come to trust these clean, easy-to-read love stories about contemporary people, set in exciting foreign places."
—*Best Sellers*, New York

Under Moonglow

by

ANNE HAMPSON

Harlequin Books

TORONTO • LONDON • NEW YORK • AMSTERDAM • SYDNEY

Original hardcover edition published in 1978
by Mills & Boon Limited

ISBN 0-373-02182-8

Harlequin edition published July 1978

CHAPTER ONE

HALF an island! The three words pivoted round in Reyna's consciousness the moment she opened her eyes. It wasn't true—none of this was true! The great four-poster bed she was in, the rough-hewn beams, the whitewashed walls all askew ... and that crazy old man with a crutch and a black patch over one eye! She had dreamt it; it was what came of reading that story to the kids at school the other day. Pirates and smugglers! All Jimmy Lloyd's fault. Last week it had been Dick Turpin, but a highwayman wasn't bloodthirsty enough for Jimmy. Oh, no, not a nice quick popping off someone with a gun; Jimmy wanted a story about pirates chopping off heads with their cutlasses and capturing coral islands where at dead of night they buried their loot——

Coral islands, pirates, loot ...

It *was* true! She, Reyna Chapman, was the owner of half of the island of Surcoufe where, said Patch, you could step ashore like the pirates of old and explore deep caves and coral coves, wander through shady cedar forests or stroll beneath the palms which fringed the white sandy beach. You could swim in the lagoon, go down and explore the fantastic coral gardens, or you could pick coconuts and mangoes and other tropical fruits and eat them straight from the trees. You could even hunt for the legendary treasure left by the pirates about two hundred years ago. It was buried somewhere in the hinterland of the island and was worth no less than thirty million pounds, declared Patch.

'Surcoufe's uninhabited except for this eccentric I've mentioned,' he had told her, his one good eye boring fiercely into her. 'Thor Granville, who's cut himself off from the rest of humanity and lives there with a dog, two giant tortoises, a cat and a tame minah bird.'

He was certainly an odd character, thought Reyna, to be living all alone like that on a small island in the Indian Ocean. And Patch's description of him was scarcely encouraging either, although Reyna rather thought that Patch exaggerated when he described the man's features as hawk-like, his eyes as tigerish and his brows as satanic.

Satanic eyebrows . . . ? Reyna had repeated to herself. Now what in the world were those?

'He's tall and spare and brown as an Arab,' Patch had continued. 'He's autocratic, with an unapproachable air about him and a lamentable lack of good manners. His mastery of words is formidable, his tongue biting and sarcastic; added to this he has a temper inherited from the devil and he's derisive of women.'

'Indeed?' Reyna had murmured, quite unable to reason out why this last little bit had sharpened her interest.

'Yes, indeed! He has a unique logic of his own regarding the place of women in the world.'

'He has?' A glint in Reyna's eyes now which any one of her class of thirty-five children would have recognised. 'And where is that, Mr Harper?'

'Back there.' He and Reyna were dining in the restaurant of the Mermaid Inn at Rye and he thumbed towards the door through which the waiters were passing back and forth. 'The kitchen. Or maybe the nursery,' inserted the old man as an afterthought.

The kitchen or the nursery, Reyna was thinking as she slid from the bed and put her feet into her slippers. A man like Thor Granville ought to be put in *his* place!

But, thought Reyna with a frown, she was not the one to do it. Pity, though; she would have liked to go to Surcoufe and 'plague' the man, as Patch wanted her to. But the most sensible thing she could do was to tell Patch, when she joined him at breakfast in about half an hour, that she had changed her mind. She would tell him that she had a pleasant job, a comfortable maisonette not far from the school where she taught, a small car and one or two very good friends. And although she had no real ties, such as a fiancé or anything like that, she did have a boy-friend now whom she liked quite a lot and with whom she might one day fall in love. She was only twenty-three, though, so she felt there was no desperate hurry. Yes, she would tell the old man all this, explaining that she had had second thoughts about accepting his most generous offer of the gift, as she could not really see how half an island, situated down there, four degrees south of the Equator, would be of very much use to her.

Having reached this decision, Reyna was soon relaxing in the bath. Yes, this delightful higgledy-piggledy medieval inn did have modern bathrooms installed, and although Reyna had to admit that it would have been more fitting if she were forced to conduct her toilet in a hip-bath, she was profoundly grateful to the proprietors of the hotel for the luxury she was at present enjoying.

After coming out of the bath she wrapped herself in the towel and stood before the long mirror rubbing herself down, and at the same time paying critical attention to her reflection. Big, limpid eyes of harebell blue; skin pale and with that subtle translucence of alabaster. The contours of her face, declared her boy-friend, had 'been etched by nature at its most superb'. Her forehead was high and unlined above delicately curving brows, her thick curling lashes were dark, unlike her hair, which was a cascade of honey-gold tinged with something akin to sunshine.

She continued to rub herself down, her thoughts naturally returning to last evening and the way she had been coerced into accepting the old man's gift. Yes, he had almost bullied her when she refused, glaring at her with his one good eye and thumping his crutch on the floor of the hotel lounge so that everyone turned to stare at the ill-assorted couple sitting there, with their drinks, at a small oak table by the massive open fireplace where pine logs burned merrily, adding their flickering light to that of the candles and the muted light coming from somewhere under the velvet-covered pelmets. Reyna supposed she had accepted the gift in order to calm the man down, because, at nintey-seven, he ought not to be getting himself into a towering rage like that.

It had all begun, reflected Reyna as she dropped the towel and used the perfumed talc, when her colleague, Janie Drake, had come into the staffroom holding a little brochure.

'You like old things and places,' she had said, dropping the brochure on to Reyna's lap as she sat sipping her coffee and subconsciously listening to the children in the playground, two of whom seemed to be having some kind of a private war. 'Why don't you spend your half-term break there? You were saying you'd be at a loose end as your boyfriend will be working. I discovered the place at the weekend when I went off in my car, just driving without any fixed destination as I often do. I found myself in Rye, saw a funny little cobbled street and drove up it. The Mermaid Inn was there, something out of another age, Reyna! The atmosphere's terrific! First, this cobbled street with its terraced houses all superbly renovated yet retaining all the charm they ever had in the old days when smugglers used them. Then this medieval inn which also has connections with smugglers; they used to bring in their booty at the port at Rye——'

'I've heard of this Mermaid Inn,' interrupted the headmaster. 'But I've never got down to going there. It must be very old, because I believe it was rebuilt some time in the fourteen-hundreds.'

'Tell me some more about it, Janie,' invited Reyna, who was interestedly perusing the brochure.

'I went in just to quench my thirst and have a look around, but found myself booking a dinner and asking for a room. I dined in the most delightful olde-worlde atmosphere with beams and brass and toby jugs and a lovely log fire. My bedroom had beams and topsy-turvy walls and a four-poster bed.'

'You actually slept in a four-poster?'

'Yes, and jolly comfortable it was too. I shall go again in the not-too-distant future. I'm only sorry I've booked that Paris trip for my half-term break.' Janie looked at Reyna. 'You'd adore it, loving old things the way you do.'

Reyna took her advice and went off in the car, having first made sure of her accommodation by telephoning the hotel. She wanted a room with a four-poster if possible, she added, and to her delight one was available owing to a cancellation. She could have it for four nights.

The hotel was all she had imagined, and more. Her room with its wealth of beams, its massive furniture and its cretonne-curtained, latticed windows took her right into the Middle Ages, and with a sigh of contentment she settled in, unpacking her suitcase and hanging her clothes in the black oak wardrobe. A short while later, having washed and changed, and put on a long velvet dress of midnight blue which had the effect of darkening her eyes and giving them a sort of mysterious glow, she went down to the lounge to have a quiet drink before dinner. The room was fairly crowded, but she found a small vacant table and sat down. The waiter brought her a dry sherry which she sipped as she glanced around. People chatting at the bar; parties of three or four at tables, obviously waiting to go in to dinner; one or two who might be locals from the houses along the cobbled street.

And then, entering through the far door which appeared to connect with another room beyond, came the most incredible figure Reyna had ever seen in her life. Tall but with shoulders drooping a little, thin to a point where he could almost be described as skin and bone, a black patch over his right eye and a crutch under his left arm, the man seemed to have emerged from a bygone age, and, as his eye darted about the room, he might have been looking for one or other of the smugglers who were his friends. He was of course merely looking for somewhere to sit, and with a little sigh Reyna saw him coming towards the vacant chair opposite to that on which she herself was seated. She noticed a certain lack of interest among those people whom she had labelled locals, and concluded that the man was a regular customer who lived close by. His walk was a little difficult but somehow firm for all that; his knee-breeches revealed spindly legs which made the heavy boots appear totally out of place. Assuredly a ludicrous figure among the women in their long dresses and the men in their smart lounge suits.

'This anybody's chair?' he asked in a gruff, pugnacious sort of voice.

'No,' replied Reyna, thinking that although he might clash with the company he fitted to perfection the atmosphere of the inn.

'Mind if I sit down?'

'No, of course not.'

She watched him park his crutch against the table, saw him lift an imperious hand to fetch a waiter to his side. While waiting for his beer he set Reyna with a stare so fierce that she became uncomfortable. She shifted in her chair, picked up her glass and sipped her sherry. The beer arrived and was despatched in one noisy swallow. Another pint arrived without his ordering it and Reyna realised that this procedure occurred regularly, the waiter having the second pint ready. Half of this was tossed off, and then the man drew forth an evil-looking pipe from his jacket pocket.

'Mind if I smoke?'

'Not at all.'

He cut some tobacco, rubbed it between his hands, then filled the pipe.

'Pardon,' he was saying a moment later as a great cloud of smoke put a screen between him and Reyna. She was conscious of amused glances from the direction of the bar where the smart set of young men and women were drinking cocktails. The men laughed with their eyes; their girl-friends giggled behind well-manicured hands or dainty lace-edged handkerchiefs. The man with the patch saw none of this; he wouldn't have been in the least concerned if he had.

'Nice place, this,' he said, and it seemed that there was a challenge in his voice as though he was daring her to argue with him on this point.

'Very nice. It has a superb atmosphere.'

'Bound to have,' he returned aggressively. 'Look at its history.'

Reyna said nothing, merely picking up her glass again and sipping her sherry.

'You alone?' demanded the man, and Reyna nodded.

'Yes.'

'Why?' asked the man disconcertingly.

She blinked.

'I like being alone at times,' she said.

'Not natural for a pretty young girl like you!' He lifted his tankard and the second half pint was quaffed as swiftly as the first. 'On holiday?' he wanted to know as he placed the tankard on the table.

'Yes; just for a few days.'

'Funny time of the year to be on holiday.'

'I teach, and it happens to be the February half-term break.'

'What do you teach? Geography?'

'No particular subject. My children are only eight to nine years old. But,' she added because, for some quite unfathomable reason, she felt it would please him, 'my main subject at College was geography.'

'Ah ... then you know where places are in the world?'

'Many places, but by no means all, I'm afraid.'

'Know the Indian Ocean?'

'I know the countries that are around it, and in it.'

'The Seychelles?'

'Of course.'

'How many islands are there in the group, then?'

What was this? wondered Reyna in some amusement. A general knowledge quiz?

'I believe there are about ninety.'

'Eighty-seven ... and I own half of one of them.'

'You do?' Reyna successfully hid her amusement as she added, 'How interesting.'

'Don't believe me, eh?' He threw out an arm to fetch the waiter. 'Do I or don't I own half an island?'

The waiter smiled, glancing at Reyna whose expression was now one of mild interest.

'It's true,' said the waiter. 'He owns half of the island of Surcoufe, which is in the Seychelles group.'

'Told you,' said the man. And, to the waiter, 'I'm having dinner tonight. Hope you haven't forgotten that it's Saturday and I always treat myself to dinner, bed and breakfast here?'

'None of us ever forgets, sir.'

'Sir, eh? For this young lady's benefit.' The one brilliant blue eye twinkled for a second. 'You can call me Patch, as you usually do; I'm not troubled about preserving my dignity, not at ninety-seven!'

'Ninety-seven!' ejaculated Reyna before she could stop herself.

'Yes! And don't say I don't look it, because I know I do! Anyway, I *want* to look it! I wish I'd been born two hundred years ago! I'm out of my time.'

That was true, Reyna agreed mentally.

'Why do you want to look your age?' she asked, and added, feeling rather daring as she did so, 'Whatever you say to the contrary, you really do not look ninety-seven.'

He glowered at her.

'Have you ever met anyone who has ninety-seven years to their credit?' he demanded.

'Well, no, but——'

'Then don't talk nonsense!' He stopped abruptly, and for the second time the blue eye twinkled. 'Sorry, miss. I'm not usually as rude as that—not quite!'

She found herself laughing. A few minutes earlier she had been debating on whether she would move, but had felt it would not look very nice if she did so. Now, however, she was becoming so intrigued with this man who owned half an island that she had not the least desire to move.

'It's all right,' she said. 'I shouldn't have said what I did, but you do have such things as excellent hearing and an alert mind, and so I expect I thought you were younger.'

'But you said I *looked* younger, which is different. And for your information, I've got most of my own teeth.' He paused, but as Reyna said nothing he added, 'Do you know how old my father was when he died?'

'I gather that he was very old.'

'A hundred and two! We're a long-lived family. Pirate Harper, my great-grandfather, buried a thirty-million-pound treasure on Surcoufe. He lived to be over a hundred and his son lived to be ninety-eight. So you can see how close I am to Pirate Harper. I remember my grandfather, who was his son.'

'Yes,' murmured Reyna obligingly when she saw that some comment was expected of her. But what exactly was the man getting at? she wondered bewilderedly. He was still looking fiercely at her and she added, 'Have you any children, Mr ... ?'

'Harper, of course. No, I haven't, and that's the tragedy!

An unbroken line from Pirate Harper to me. And when I've gone there's no one to take over the half of Surcoufe and look for the treasure. That scamp who's bought the other half's living there as if he owns the lot! And searching every day of his life for the treasure, which he'll confiscate! He knows I'm too old to fight him, the brute! If I had children or grandchildren—— But I haven't, so he thinks he's going to come in for the lot——'

'Excuse me, madam, but you can go in for dinner any time you like.'

'Thank you,' returned Reyna, glancing up at the waiter.

'We might as well have it together,' suggested Patch. 'It'll be a table for two because they haven't tables for one. Joe, see that another cover's laid on this young woman's table.'

'It's all right,' smiled Reyna as she noticed the waiter's doubtful glance. 'We'll sit together.'

'Then perhaps you'll leave it a few moments until the other cover's laid?'

'Nice of you to have me,' said Patch. 'I'm a lonely old man and sometimes I wonder what I'm going on for. Yet I can't abide the idea of dying and letting that rogue have the whole of the island!' He paused, staring at her with that fierce, glowering look that seemed to see right into her mind. He was formidable now, at ninety-seven; Reyna could not help wondering what he had been like at thirty or forty. 'I'll tell you all about it over dinner, and you'll understand just how I feel about that rat who's lording it on my half as well as his own!'

The first course was—for Reyna—oeufs mimosa, but her companion had soup. He talked a great deal and it was impossible, as she listened, that Reyna could not become profoundly interested in this amazing story of an unspoiled coral island, and a treasure, and a recluse who lived there but was only thirty-five years of age. Young Jimmy, mused Reyna, would sit enthralled through a tale like this, as it had everything—the capture of the island by Pirate Harper and his cousin who, about two hundred years ago, stormed Surcoufe and slaughtered the band of pirates who were already in possession, the burying of a vast amount of gold and other booty, the killing and robbing of other pirates who came afterwards.

Pirate Harper and his cousin had shared the island between them, each claiming half but not, apparently, having any clear line of demarcation drawn up. However, it would appear that some sort of deeds did eventually come into being, because on the death of Pirate Harper's cousin his son, who inherited the half share, sold it to a woman who lived there on her own for some years, Pirate Harper having left the island hurriedly to spend the rest of his life dodging the law. His son lived on the island for a time, searching for the treasure, and during this period Patch's father was born.

Meanwhile, the other half was sold again, then given away to a young, newly-married couple who stayed for over fifty years. By some mistake which this couple made in the boundary, their house was built on the half owned by Patch's grandfather, but he didn't seem to mind. But when they sold their half eventually, their house could not go with it. It was the half of the island owned by this couple that had come into Thor Granville's possession, and from what Reyna could gather, this unpleasant person had immediately begun to harass poor old Patch because he wanted to buy his half.

'He wanted the treasure,' declared Patch, viciously thumping the table with his fist. 'I wasn't going to let him have it, so I refused to sell. He turned nasty and I had to come away from Surcoufe in the end, which gave him great satisfaction, no doubt! I decided to sell to someone else, just to spite the rogue—who was fully expecting to get my half in a short while because of my age.' The one blue eye glittered with fury as Patch went on to tell Reyna that after he had advertised his half of Surcoufe he had dozens of replies.

'These prospective purchasers all wanted to see the island, naturally, and that villain put them all off by saying that any proposed developments would be objected to by him and that he would approach the government for a preservation order for the island. He also said that even if they were allowed to develop for tourism no road would be allowed on his half of Surcoufe—no sort of development at all! Well, the division's such that nothing can be done unless you have co-operation from Granville, so I couldn't make a sale. The trickster then made another offer for my share, but I told him to go to h—to the devil!' Patch drew a loud, furious breath. 'He'll get it, of course! When I'm gone the island and the treasure will fall into his hands entirely!'

'What a shame,' frowned Reyna, deciding that Thor Granville was one of those people whose one concern in life was that of amassing money. It was plain that, once he got possession of the island, either he himself would develop it, building hotels and casinos and hacking down the lovely trees to make roads all over the place, or he would sell out and make a few million pounds in the process. She seethed at the idea, mentally wishing she could do something to prevent the man succeeding in his nefarious plans. To harass a poor old man like that!

'Were you living on Surcoufe permanently?' she asked as the thought occurred to her and she saw, in her mind's eye, Patch being driven off his own property. But he shook his head.

'Not permanently,' he answered. 'I went over several times, just to make sure he hadn't yet discovered the treasure. He'd been digging, though. I accused him of it and he said it was the dog, burying bones! Have you ever heard an excuse like that?'

'No, indeed,' returned Reyna hotly. What a pity Patch didn't have anyone to leave his property to. 'How long is it since you were there last?'

'Three months—— Oh, yes, I'm quite capable of taking the flight, and the boat trip. I enjoyed it and would have stayed, but he made me so uncomfortable that I had to come away after only two days there.'

He looked so sad, thought Reyna, although that fierce expression could never be erased; it was an inherent part of him which, she suspected, had come right down from the bloodthirsty Pirate Harper himself.

'He certainly sounds detestable. It's no wonder you and he are bitter enemies.' Reyna had no doubt, though, that the treasure which was so troublesome to Patch did not exist and therefore Thor Granville was wasting his time in digging for it. If it ever had existed it would be gone by now in any case, as someone would surely have found it. She mentioned this to Patch, but he shook his head emphatically, pointing out that few people had lived on the island during the past two hundred years.

'Only four families—and you can't call that woman living on her own a family. She wasn't interested in looking for the fortune anyway; she was interested only in her animals, and when she died she said that none of the dozens of cats and dogs she had kept there must be killed.'

'Then there must be hundreds of dogs and cats there now!'

'They were removed. The person who bought the half she owned got rid of the lot.'

The second course came, delicious rainbow trout meunière for Reyna and roast beef for Patch. He talked a lot, some of which was irrelevant, but much of which was still of interest to Reyna. She felt sorry that he had not been able to sell his half of the island; it would have afforded him immense satisfaction to have thwarted that disagreeable man who, it was plain, felt himself to be the owner of the whole of Surcoufe. She asked about his life there, imagining him to be living in some shack, in a rather Robinson Crusoe manner.

Apparently it was not like that at all. Thor Granville was obviously a man of means, since he had built himself a lovely villa and surrounded himself with every luxury and modern convenience, making his own electricity. So she had been wrong in her assumption that his intention was to sell the island. It seemed that the man was intending to make it his permanent home. His intention, then, was to develop it himself, keeping the hotels well away from his own house. She had to smile at her mind-wanderings. She was building up a picture that could prove to be all wrong. What was certainly not likely to be proved wrong was the sheer wickedness of the man who was out to rob Patch—or at least, to get his greedy hands on Patch's property one day in the not-so-distant future. For it was unlikely that a man of ninety-seven had much longer to go.

'How does he get his supplies?' she asked. 'How did he manage to build this villa you mention?'

'The island's remote, but by no means totally isolated. As you know, the Seychelles are scattered, but many of the islands are within easy reach of Victoria, the capital. Surcoufe's about two and a half hours' journey by boat from Victoria.'

'The boats call with supplies, then?'

'Once a fortnight, yes.'

'How long has Thor Granville been there?'

'Three years.' Patch ground his teeth. 'The shark!' he rasped.

'You obviously dislike him intensely, Mr Harper.'

'I hate him! I wish it were possible to take up a cutlass and swipe off his arrogant head!'

The blue eye stared fiercely into space. It was as well for this man Thor Granville that Patch was old, and that he no longer wanted to go and live on Surcoufe. For Reyna had little difficulty in seeing Thor Granville lying there with his throat cut, or sprawled on the rocks with the waves washing over his lifeless body. Yes, she mused as she watched

Patch's face twist among its numberless lines and wrinkles, the man could kill without compunction, she felt sure.

When at last the meal was over Patch suggested they return to the lounge; he would like to buy her a drink before he went to bed. They found a table near the fire and sat down, Patch once again propping up his crutch against the table. He began talking about the island and it was plain that the thought of its going to his enemy was giving him a great deal of mental anguish.

'Why don't you advertise it again?' suggested Reyna. 'Or you could put it in the hands of an estate agent who deals with overseas properties.'

'It isn't any use. That man'll continue to put everyone off. He knows he has the advantage of me, because I'm old, and have no one to fight my battles for me ...' His voice trailed off to silence and Reyna's heart was touched by his unhappiness. What an unscrupulous scoundrel that Thor Granville was to make this poor old man's last years so miserable! She felt sure that, had he treated Patch more kindly, he would have had no trouble in persuading him to sell, but it was obvious that the man was optimistic enough to believe he would get it for a song when Patch died, as it was left to charity, Patch had earlier mentioned. On his death it would be sold, and as Thor Granville would be the only person interested in buying it, then it was reasonable to assume that he would get it for a great deal less than it was worth.

Once again Reyna seethed. She had always been affected by injustice, and she was certainly affected now. She felt that if she had the money she would even consider buying the property, and going over there to give the detestable Thor Granville a dose of his own medicine! Yes, she would give him troubles in plenty, pretending that she intended to develop her half for tourism. She would talk of turning it into another Blackpool! That would shake him, and keep him awake at nights. Reyna's visions continued to come

thick and fast, born of her anger against Thor Granville on
the one hand and her pity for the old man on the other. But
at last she turned her thoughts into less impossible chan-
nels, suggesting to Patch that he should not despair, but
keep persevering as he was bound to find a buyer one day.

But he seemed to have fallen into the deep gloom of
pessimism. He went on about 'that scamp', declaring that
he would soon be dead but that he would never rest in his
grave until Thor Granville was dead too.

'Don't get like this, Mr Harper,' begged Reyna in distress. 'Let me buy you a drink.'

'All right.' He lapsed into gloom again, mumbling something about wishing he had a relative who would 'plague'
the man, mumbling on about other things, and as she listened Reyna learned that he had been married twice and had
had one child, a daughter who died when she was three days
old. By this time Reyna was sinking into the depths of
gloom herself, wishing with all her heart that she could
think of some way in which she could cheer him up.

'You *will* sell it,' she asserted, because she could think of
nothing else to say. Patch was shaking his head.

'No ... But ...' He raised his head and looked at her
hard and long with that fierce blue eye of his. 'By Jove! It's
fate! Meeting you is fate!' His whole manner had changed
with miraculous suddenness. Reyna, startled, could only
stare at him, waiting to hear what this was all about. 'I
can't sell it but, by heaven, I can give it away!'

'Give it away?' she echoed. 'Who to?'

'Why, you, of course!'

Reyna put a finger to her breast and stammered,

'To—to m-me, Mr Harper?'

'Why not? You've shown me that you dislike that rat as
much as I! And so——'

'Not as much as you, Mr Harper, because you see, I
haven't even met him.' Her mind was so dazed that she
scarcely knew what she was saying. She had a vague idea

somewhere deep in her subconscious that she must refuse this offer, but for some reason the words to voice this refusal did not come as swiftly as they should have done.

'Well, you *will* meet him and then you'll know what a rascal he is! Just think, he's gloating out there where he's living as if he were Lord of Surcoufe! Gloating because he has me beaten! But here am I, plotting to beat him! My, but Pirate Harper would be proud of me if he knew!'

Patch seemed to be raving, but quietly, which was surprising, so much vehemence was he putting into his words. Reyna, her mind passing through a series of chaotic emotions, was for the present beyond coping with the situation. She was fascinated by the change in Patch; he seemed to be right on top of the world, his thin colourless mouth curved in a smile, which was the first she had seen, and his eye was alive with something far different from the fury which seemed never to have left its depths since the moment he had first mentioned the island.

She listened as he continued, talking as though she already owned half of Surcoufe and was intending to go there and harass the arrogant, possessive owner of the other half. He stopped at last—for breath, decided Reyna with a wry expression. He looked wicked, really wicked, sitting there, his blue eye glinting, the thin bloodless lips tight now, and cruel. Reyna tried to imagine him in his youth, but also living in the age to which he belonged—the age of adventure and fearlessness, when buccaneering men were brave and cruel, when murder was almost a sport among the pirates, when the acquiring of gold was paramount in the minds of these wild sea-rovers—yet what they did with their loot other than bury it seemed to remain a mystery. Wherever there was an island associated with pirates, there was bound to be a story of treasure buried somewhere on that island.

'Mr Harper,' managed Reyna at last, 'I can't accept your very generous offer. I'm a stranger to you——'

'Stranger! No, you're not! Don't you believe in fate? No matter—I do, and we were destined to meet so that I could get this damned worry off my mind! Go there if you can. Spend all your holidays there. Plague him, make a thorough nuisance of yourself! Take all your young friends and turn the place into a holiday camp. Let them run wild——'

'Please . . . I can't accept this gift. There must be someone else you can give it too——'

'Plenty of people, now that the idea of giving it away has come to me, but they'd sell it! You won't; I know you won't because you're an honourable person who'll always be conscious of the reason why I gave it to you—so that *he* could be thwarted, so that he'll never get hold of the other half as long as he lives!' He was exhausting himself, and Reyna was troubled by the purple colouring that had crept into his wrinkled cheeks. 'Perhaps you won't be able to go there yet awhile, but you will eventually. We'll go on Monday morning to my solicitors and have it signed over to you——'

'I can't accept it,' she cried, wishing her mind would clear, for in this muddled state she was quite likely to do something she would come to regret. There must be all sorts of problems attached to owning half an island. There might be enormous taxes put on her one day, or some kind of conditions ordered by the government. Her life was nice and smooth; she wanted to keep it that way. 'If you give it to someone else you can stipulate that they mustn't ever sell it to Mr Granville——'

'They'd get round a clause like that! No, it's got to be a matter of conscience, and you have a conscience. I'm definitely giving it to you, Miss——' He stopped. 'I don't know your name, do I?'

It was absurd, but Reyna had an hysterical desire to laugh. Here was this old man, offering to make her a gift of half an island, and he didn't even know her name! She gave it to him but doubted if he heard, so preoccupied had he become.

'What a shock he's going to get! I'll have my solicitors send him a cable on Monday morning—and I'll wager he doesn't get a wink of sleep for weeks! Thwarted! He'll be gnashing his teeth.' Patch looked at her gleefully. 'A woman too! And him with his opinion of them! He'll go raving mad when he learns that it's a woman who owns the other half!' He was working himself up, and Reyna became anxious in case he should collapse.

'Please, Mr Harper, try to understand that I can't accept. I won't accept!' she stated emphatically, catching her breath as she saw his frenzied expression. If he did collapse and it was fatal, she would feel like a murderess. 'Try to understand——' The rest was lost as he thumped his crutch on the floor.

'I shall make you accept! It's ridiculous for you to refuse! What about all that treasure? It could be yours! I shall make you accept, so you might as well accept now— now, I say!' His breath seemed to be failing him; Reyna glanced around helplessly, aware that people were paying a great deal of attention to the old man. She hesitated; then, taking another frightened look at him, she heard herself saying, in a soothing, placatory tone of voice,

'Don't excite yourself any more, Mr Harper. I'll accept.

CHAPTER TWO

AFTER coming from the bathroom Reyna put on dainty
underwear, then a pleated skirt of heather-mixture tweed,
and a Shetland wool sweater with a classical neckline. She
brushed her hair, touched her lips with colour, then drew
on a tailor-made jacket which matched the skirt. The white
leather shoulder bag matched the sweater and also the
flower spray of costume jewellery which she wore in the
lapel of her jacket. A touch of perfume on her wrists and
behind her ears, a glance in the mirror to make sure she
was looking her usual bright self and she was ready to go
down to breakfast. But her mind was a little troubled. She
wondered how Patch was going to take the news that she
had changed her mind. She could never have done it last
night, indeed no—not with him being in that over-excited
state. She hoped he would be calmer this morning—even
hoped that he was regretting his offer and therefore would
be only too glad that she had changed her mind. Yes, if he
was regretting his offer it would be the best thing that
could have happened.

She left the bedroom after taking an appreciative glance
around which gave her the pleasant picture of the great oak
bed with its lace drapes, the ancient furniture, the crooked
walls and the highly-polished floorboards that squeaked
alarmingly when walked upon. Delightful! She would
always be grateful to Janie for recommending the hotel to
her.

She went along the corridor whose floor sloped so crazily
that she had the sensation of walking downhill; the stairs
twisted and turned within their black oak balustrades, their
treads protesting violently beneath the turkey red carpeting

that covered them. Reyna was at last standing at the open door of the dining-room. The old man was already there and she stood for a moment, unobserved, and found herself suppressing laughter. He was unreal, this age-weathered buccaneer! He was sitting with his back to the massive fireplace, his crutch propped against the table, one eye covered with the black patch, the other glowering at the menu which he held at arms' length.

He glanced up, noticed her and produced a bright smile. He would not be smiling soon, though, when she told him she didn't want his share of the island. He beckoned imperiously with a long bony finger and she moved towards the table, aware of the waiter—a different one from the young man who had served them last night—standing there, looking curiously from her to Patch and back again. She slipped out of her jacket after placing her bag on a spare chair; the waiter was there to take her jacket and drape it over the back of the vacant chair. She gave him a smile, murmured 'good morning', then turned her attention to the old man sitting there.

'Good morning, Mr Harper. I hope you slept well?'

·Morning to you, Reyna. Yes, I had the best night for some time—in spite of the ghosts,' he added for the benefit of the waiter who was standing by, ready to take their orders.

Reyna laughed.

'I must admit this place makes you think of ghosts,' she agreed. 'And as a matter of fact I had hopes of seeing one. But alas, no such luck!' She sat down and picked up the menu. 'Grapefruit juice, bacon, eggs and toast, please. And coffee.' She glanced at Patch inquiringly.

'No kippers,' he grunted fractiously.

·They smell,' frowned Reyna.

'You wouldn't have enjoyed your breakfast if I'd had had kippers?'

'I'm afraid not. The smell of kippers at this time of the

day is too much for me.' She paused a moment, debating on whether she should speak now, and get it over and done with, or wait until after breakfast. Wait, she decided. Let the poor old man enjoy his meal—if he could enjoy it, that was, with there being no kippers.

He said, as she was drinking her fruit juice,

'Try to go over if you can, won't you? It will remind Granville that the island doesn't belong to him alone.'

Reyna said nothing. He had not changed his mind as she had hoped. What must she do? A short while ago it was all clear in her mind: she would not accept—could not do so because she and Patch were strangers. You didn't accept the gift of all that land from someone you didn't know, and for the reasons he had given. Now, however, she was in a state of indecision. Why should she disappoint him? It was easy to see that he was deriving extreme satisfaction and pleasure from his thoughts. He could see his enemy's fury and frustration on discovering that he would never now be able to gain possession of the other half of the island. Perhaps the old man was even picturing Thor Granville's departure from Surcoufe altogether, since he would be unable to continue living there once his plans had gone awry.

They had their breakfast; Patch was happy, with a tranquillity about his manner which, Reyna suspected, had not been there for some considerable time.

She ate her eggs and bacon, buttered her toast and spread marmalade on it, and all the time she was rehearsing what she had already rehearsed in her bedroom. Yet when the meal was over and the words were ready to be uttered her pity rose once more and she knew she could not bring the old man down to the depths again. A sigh escaped her; what was she letting herself in for? The problems of being a landowner seemed to mount alarmingly in her imagination. There was no income from the land, so any expenses that might be incurred at any time would have to be paid out of her own pocket ...

'Oh, dear!' The words were another long-drawn-out sigh and her companion glanced at her perceptively.

'You've had second thoughts,' he said, and it was a statement, not a question. She bit her lip, automatically nodding.

'I felt you might. You're such a conscientious young lady. I knew it, as I said. You feel it's wrong to take my half of the island—but you haven't really stopped to think. Is it any use to me? That's one question which you can answer easily. Last evening you were frightened; I can tell you now that I've had an idea that my end isn't too far away. The old heart must be giving out after ninety-seven years, mustn't it? While I do live, though, this half of Surcoufe's a burden to me—because of that thief who's got the other half. If you take it I shall end my days in peace, but even if you don't take it, I shan't be too unhappy, not now that I've met you and know that you're straight and honest and wouldn't let me down.' He paused, noticing her puzzled expression. 'You see,' he continued slowly and emphatically, 'I've decided that if you won't accept the property as a gift then you'll accept it as a legacy.'

'A ... legacy?' Reyna shook her head protestingly, even while it was running through her mind that she really could not prevent him from making her his beneficiary. He had her name; she had told him where she came from and mentioned the school at which she taught. 'I don't——'

'The choice is yours,' he interrupted. 'But I'll tell you here and now that I intend you to have my half of Surcoufe, because I can then be absolutely sure that it will never belong to that scoundrel!'

Reyna looked at him, half wishing she had never come to this place ... and yet it could have been fate. For it was within her power to make this man happy, this lonely old man who had been treated só badly by that rogue, Thor Granville. She spoke at last, saying quietly,

'I think I will accept, Mr Harper, but could you please

give me a little time to consider? It's all been such a—well, a shock to me. I feel that's the only word I can use to describe your very generous offer——'

'Not generous,' he broke in. 'Selfish—as I'm thinking only of myself and you know it!'

Yes, she did know it, but the offer still seemed a generous one. The problems she had previously thought of loomed up again, but she ignored them. Time enough to worry about such things later.

'How long do you want?' asked Patch at length.

'A week ... ?'

He nodded his head.

'That'll be fine. I'll give you my address, and the address of my solicitors. When you've made up your mind you just telephone them and arrange to come down and we can have it all signed over to you.'

She had to smile at the way he had taken for granted her acceptance while he still lived. He probably guessed that she wanted to make him as happy as possible.

'I'll do that,' she promised, and a short while later she was standing on the cobblestones outside the inn watching him as he went down the narrow street. Her eyes became dreamy; she was trying to imagine that island, with the palms waving on its beach, the lagoon and the reef ... and then the only blot on the enchanting vision, Thor Granville, detestable owner of half the island.

Four days later she was called into the headmaster's study to receive a telephone call. It was from a Mr Stephen Gatley of Briggs, Gatley and Naughton, solicitors, of Rye in Sussex. Mr Ignatius Harper had died peacefully in his sleep last evening.

'Bad news?' asked the Head with a troubled frown.

Reyna swallowed hard, feeling foolish because there were tears in her eyes for a man she didn't really know. He had died peacefully. She was glad about that.

'Not really,' she replied. She had not mentioned anything of her adventure to any of the staff, merely enthusing on the merits of the inn and recommending it just as Janie had done. 'But I have to go to Rye——' She paused, looking at him. 'Is it possible for me to have a day off school, Mr Wyman?'

'Of course. I can take your class myself for one day. Are you sure it's not bad news, Miss Chapman?'

She shook her head, and found herself saying,

'A—a friend has—has died and I have to see a solicitor.'

'I see ... Rye—that's a strange coincidence, as you were there for the half-term break, weren't you?'

'Yes.' She was more upset than she would have believed, wishing now that she had not asked for a week's grace but had given Patch her decision right away—or rather, kept to the decision she had already made.

'I could have had it as a gift,' she was saying to Stephen Gatley the following morning as she sat in his office in High Street. 'I wish now that I had.'

'We heard all about it, Miss Chapman. He was a very odd character with this obsession about Mr Granville and this conviction that there's buried treasure on Surcoufe. He came in here at nine o'clock on Monday morning and insisted we make out another will there and then. He refused to budge from Mr Briggs' office until it was all done and signed. He seemed extraordinarily happy at the idea of your having his half of the island. In fact, I myself have never seen him happy at all until then.' He looked at her and smiled into his beard. 'He said that he hoped you would take the property as a gift, but he was making his will out in your favour anyway. There's some money——'

'Money!' exclaimed Reyna, distressed. 'Oh, I can't take the money! It wouldn't be right at all!'

The young man smiled again, his eyes appreciative as they settled on her face for a moment.

'There isn't much—about four hundred or so. If you

don't take it, Miss Chapman, then where will it go?'

She shrugged her shoulders.

'I have no idea. Mr Gatley, I *can't* take money that shouldn't be mine!'

'Well, I suggest you speak to Mr Briggs about that part of it. I will say, though, that Mr Harper expressed the wish that you would use the money to take the trip out to Surcoufe ...'

It was three weeks later that Reyna received the letter from the solicitors at Rye. It was a short note to explain that the enclosed letter had come to them from Mr Thor Granville, who had requested that they pass it on to her.

She was in the sitting-room of her pretty, well-furnished little home, and as it was Saturday she was not in any rush to be getting her breakfast ready. She opened the envelope and withdrew the single sheet of paper it contained, and as her eyes scanned the lines she found herself recalling Patch's assertion that Thor Granville had a formidable mastery of words. Well, he certainly did not believe in wasting any, that was for sure!

The address was written at the top of the page: Villa Surcoufe, Surcoufe, Seychelles.

'Madam,

You have come into property which, being of no practical value to you, will no doubt be up for sale. I am willing to negotiate for the purchase of this property, and suggest you have your solicitors contact mine at the address given below. A speedy transaction will no doubt be arranged.

Thor Granville.'

'Well!' exclaimed Reyna as she read, 'the cheek of the man!' Her blood boiled as she read it again, picking out words and phrases. No practical value ... How did he know it was of no value to her? She might just decide to go and live there! He was willing to negotiate ... Not *anxious* to negotiate! Arrogant, dictatorial creature! 'And he *suggests* I have my solicitors contact his! That word, suggests, savours very much of an order to me.'

Reyna screwed up the sheet of paper into a tiny ball and tossed it into the waste-paper basket. But, later, she retrieved it and wrote in answer,

'Sir,
You have been misinformed about my property. It is of great value to me in that I might decide to make my permanent home on Surcoufe. From what I have been told by my very good friend, Mr Harper, there seems to be an important potential regarding development for tourism. A few inquiries as to the reaction of the authorities in Mahé will be made in the immediate future and if permission is granted building will commence immediately. Should you not care for the idea of development, you might like to put your half of the island up for sale, in which case I could probably arrange a speedy transaction for its purchase.
Reyna Chapman.'

She felt much better for having written that. And in case she should be troubled by the half-lies she had told, she went out immediately after breakfast and posted the letter.

'That's that! Patch, I hope you approve!'

The next thing Reyna did was to write to the solicitors accepting the money Patch had left her. She was intending to take a trip to the Seychelles some time during her summer vacation.

'Why the Seychelles?' Reyna's boy-friend asked with a frown when she told him of her plans. 'That's a long way to go for a fortnight.'

'I have to go, Kevin,' she said. 'It's a private matter, so please don't ask me about it.' She had still not mentioned her inheritance to anyone except her aunt. Kevin was not in her confidence simply because she had not known him long enough to confide her private affairs. She liked him, enjoying the outings they had together, but she had—at present—no feeling for him other than friendship. She had not confided in her colleagues, either. There would be too many questions involving answers which must inevitably sound too fantastic to be true. But Reyna had told her Aunt Saran about the island, and the detestable man who was at present in sole possession. Reyna's aunt had brought her up from the age of nine when her parents had died in a train disaster. Aunt Saran's real names were Sarah Ann, but Reyna had begun to shorten them from the time she was able to talk and now the original names had almost been forgotten by Reyna, and even her aunt would sign personal letters with the shortened version of her names.

'Half an island!' Aunt Saran had exclaimed disbelievingly when her niece had told her the whole story. 'Are you serious, child?'

Reyna laughed.

'I can prove it! Come with me when I go over. I might need an ally,' she added with a grimace.

'If it had been later in the year I would have come, but as you know I've to take my holidays this year in September. You'll be back at school by then.'

'Yes. Never mind, you might be able to come with me next year.'

'You're going again next year?' Aunt Saran's merry grey eyes twinkled. 'You might have had enough with your visit this time. I don't like the sound of that man at all. I hope, dear, that you're not intending to sleep on the island?'

'No. As I told you, Auntie, I've been making inquiries and I've discovered from the travel agent that boats will call there any day if you make arrangements beforehand. Normally, only one boat a fortnight calls, but this is only because Mr Granville's stopped the others from calling. Apparently, at one time when there was no one living on the island at all, a few people brought their boats in and explored the beaches, and had picnics. Thor Granville stopped all that and now he has only one boat a fortnight bringing his supplies. But boats are moving around among the various islands and if you make arrangements you can get the captain to put you off and pick you up on his way back. I shall stay in Victoria—in fact my hotel's already booked. I plan to go over every day to the island, just to let Mr Thor Granville know that I have as much right on Surcoufe as he has.'

'Well, it sounds safe enough.' Aunt Saran admitted. 'But watch yourself.'

'He hates women in general and he'll already be hating me in particular. I'll be safe enough, Aunt Saran, so don't you start worrying yourself, will you?'

'Well, I'll try not to. You've always been capable of taking care of yourself.'

'And I'll manage to take care of myself on Surcoufe. I'll be as safe there as I am here with you, darling!'

'You're very trusting. A man and a woman on a tropical island spells temptation with a capital T!'

Reyna laughed.

'You can be sure that there's nothing like *that* to fear. I guess he'd rather kill me than force his attentions on me.'

The hotel, on the island of Mahé, consisted mainly of detached bungalows, of which Reyna had one all to herself. She was driven to the hotel from the airport and the following morning at a quarter to eight she was boarding *La Belle Coralline* at the New Port, Victoria, and at eight prompt the boat sailed. It was just over two and a half hours later that Reyna was preparing to wade from the boat to the shore, rolling up her trews to her thighs. The guide in charge of the group of tourists had earlier pointed out the island, lying serenely beautiful within the confines of the horseshoe-shaped coral reef.

As the boat drew near to Surcoufe a man appeared with a large dog at his heels. Tall and angular, clad in khaki shorts and a pair of sandals, he seemed, even from this distance, to be frowning and grim. Probably he was frowning, thought Reyna as, picking up her shoes and her rucksack, she prepared to get off the boat, watched by thirty or more interested tourists taking the trip to another island where they would spend the whole day. Yes, it wouldn't be at all surprising if Thor Granville was frowning, because he was not expecting a boat to draw so close to the island. He stared, while the dog, a red-setter type but slightly larger, barked furiously as if warning the occupants of the boat that the island of Surcoufe was private property.

Gingerly, helped by a young man who supported her by putting out an arm for her to hold on to, Reyna stepped from the boat into the clear warm water. She turned, to thank the young man and to remind the guide to have the boat call for her on its way back to Victoria.

'Yes,' nodded the girl. 'It'll be around four o'clock.'

'That'll be fine.' Reyna looked across the shallow water to the man standing there, his eyes narrowed against the sun. She wondered if he had guessed who she was, and decided he would have done so even though she had not extended the courtesy of warning him of her visit. She was visiting her own property, so it had nothing to do with him anyway. She could come and go as she liked.

Excitement filled her; it had done so ever since she stepped aboard the massive jumbo jet at London Airport. It was her first really long flight and she had thoroughly enjoyed it, being fortunate in having two vacant seats next to hers, which enabled her to stretch out and get some sleep during the night. And now that the end of her journey was in sight her heart was actually thumping against her ribs. To own half a tropical island! Even the formidable Thor Granville seemed to fade into insignificance;

nothing else intruded into her mind except the fact that she was about to set foot on *her* property. Or perhaps this particular spot on the beach belonged to Thor Granville. It did not matter; she would soon be learning which part of this delectable island belonged to her.

Slowly she waded through the blue waters of the lagoon, her excitement reaching its peak as she stepped ashore, the water having come no higher than her knees. She stopped to stare at the man and for a long moment their eyes met unwaveringly. It struck Reyna at once that he might have expected an older woman, and it crossed her mind that he might already be optimistically thinking that anyone so young as she could not possibly prove to be a formidable opponent.

The dog, at a word from his master, had sat down on its haunches, but low growls could still be heard issuing from the back of his throat. Reyna took a couple of steps forward as she felt the surf roll gently over her feet. Thor Granville's eyes still fixed hers, arresting, deep-set eyes, topaz in colour but with an unusual addition of grey in their depths—steely grey. They became narrowed as they took her measure, from her gleaming honey-gold hair to her feet, with their shapely ankles and immaculately-kept toe nails, rose-pink against the sand. Little drops of water glistened on them, and on her legs. The topaz darkened in his half-closed eyes as they moved to take unhurried stock of her features.

An upsurge of anger brought a sparkle to Reyna's eyes at this intense examination of her body. She detested the man's arrogant silence, his saturnine features, his thin lips and nostrils. He was as insufferable as Patch had branded him—and more! Her glance took in his hair, tawny-brown and faintly bleached at the temples, and at the front where it was swept back ruthlessly from a high forehead. His eyebrows were straight, and darker than his hair. Satanic eye brows ... Well, that was how Patch saw them, and she was only too willing to do the same! But she could not really agree about the tigerish eyes; rather were they lazy eyes, long-lashed, and it was only the steely glints that seemed to be active.

'Good morning.' The brusque greeting came at last, spoken in cultured, finely-timbred accents that seemed at variance with the man's general appearance. Reyna's blue eyes went automatically to the shorts, which were frayed at the bottom of the legs, and to the sandals of brown leather which were very much the worse for wear. 'You, I presume, are Miss Chapman?'

Reyna inclined her head in reply and returned stiffly,

'Good morning, Mr Granville.' She paused a moment before murmuring the polite addition, 'How do you do?'

He made no answer to that and again their eyes met, a metallic brilliance in his and a glint in hers, blue and brittle as the tropical sky above.

The first spark of hostility had flared.

'I have had no notification of your intended visit to Surcoufe, Miss Chapman.' The undisguised censure in his tone caused Reyna to bristle, and there was a trace of arrogance in her own voice as she said,

'As I was visiting my own property I saw no reason why I should be obliged to notify you.' She glanced round and felt happy. There was a sort of languorous peace in the atmosphere, an element of magic in the sway of the palms fringing the shore. Other sensations and impressions came crowding in—the blue lagoon sleeping in the sunshine and the curling white frills of surf breaking over the reef; exotic perfumes hovering on the breeze and the salt-tang from the sands at her feet; unfamiliar sounds and colours—cicadas in the casuarinas and the soft stuttered cooing of a blue-grey dove in the foliage of a banyan tree, the brilliant crimson plumage of a fody as it flashed by and disappeared into the cedar forest which spread back from the shore.

Reyna drew an ecstatic breath. Did she really own half of this little piece of paradise? She looked up at the man standing some small distance from her, and suddenly she felt awkward standing there, with her shoes in her hand, her rucksack slung over one shoulder, her jeans rolled up to her thighs. She took her rucksack off, fumbled with the fastenings, then brought out a towel. She also had a complete change of clothing as, having been warned that there was no jetty on Surcoufe and therefore she would have to wade to the shore, she thought she had better be prepared for the contingency of the water being deeper than she had been led to believe. The extra outfit consisted of a pair of powder blue shorts, a short-sleeved white sun-top which was in effect a blouse, a pair of canvas sandals, and, of course, underwear.

She bent to dry her legs, then stood on the towel, removing the sand from her feet. She put on her shoes and, finally, rolled down her jeans, and felt ready to do battle with the formidable Thor Granville should that be necessary. She straightened up and said,

'I'm here to make a survey of my property with the intention of assessing its potential as a holiday resort. If you will oblige by pointing out the line of demarcation between my half of this island and yours, I'll take up no more of your time.' The voice was not her usual soft and musical one; she had adopted a brisk and businesslike tone with the deliberate intention of disabusing him, should he be cherishing any hopes that, because she was a mere female —and a young one at that—she could be easily browbeaten. Thor Granville's expression became unfathomable; he seemed to be keeping a rein on his temper only with the greatest difficulty. 'Shall we begin right away?' she added when he did not speak. 'I have only a few hours as the boat is picking me up on its way back to Victoria. It's taking some tourists to one of the other islands for the day——'

Reyna stopped, as it suddenly occurred to her that the man would know that *La Belle Coralline* was taking tourists to another island. 'I shall be coming again tomorrow, and the next day,' she said, just to let him know that his peace was about to be disturbed for a while.

'You're staying in Victoria?' he asked.

'Yes, for——' Again she stopped. Originally she had arranged to have only the first fortnight of her six weeks' holiday here in the Seychelles, but she rather thought that she might not be at all anxious to leave when the time came, in which case she would stay longer—if she could arrange her flight back to England, that was.

'Yes?' prompted Thor Granville quietly.

'I don't know how long I shall stay. It could be for six weeks.'

'Six weeks,' he frowned. 'Is there any reason for your mentioning that particular period?'

She looked at him with a puzzled expression.

'Should there be a reason?' she countered.

'There's usually a reason for a person's actions,' he returned suavely. 'It could be that six weeks is the extent of your summer vacation,' he added in a tone devoid of expression.

Reyna shot him a startled glance. Had he guessed that she worked for a living? She hoped not, seeing that it was her intention to hoodwink him into believing that she had the funds to carry out the development she had mentioned.

'Can I see the boundary?' she asked, changing the subject. 'As I've said, I haven't much time.'

Thor Granville's lazy topaz eyes held an odd expression; Reyna had the idea that he was on the verge of imparting some very important information to her and she waited, but he seemed to change his mind.

'If you'll come with me I'll try my best to point it out to you,' he said. He glanced down at the dog. 'Stay,' he ordered, and began to walk briskly in the direction of the forest.

'Can I leave my rucksack somewhere?' asked Reyna, fuming at his lack of manners in striding away like that. He stopped and turned, impatience on his face.

'Put it down there, on that rock. Shah won't touch it.'

She laid it down, the towel spread over it so that it would dry in the sun.

'I hope,' she said stiffly when they had been walking for a few moments in complete silence, 'that I'm not taking up too much of your time?'

'I can't say that it's the most convenient time for you to have come,' he answered, and Reyna instantly brought to mind Patch's assertion that Thor Granville had a lamentable lack of good manners. This was certainly true, since he was not making the slightest effort to be civil. 'It would have been more appropriate if you had acquainted me with the information that you were intending to visit Surcoufe.' How stiff and formal! Did the man ever unbend? she wondered, thinking that this was the best place for him, on an island, isolated from the rest of his kind! Pity it was such an enchanting island, though. He ought to have been somewhere more fitting to his austere personality.

'I have the map with me,' she informed him crisply. 'The solicitors gave it to me. I can perhaps manage without your help.'

'It's up to you,' was his careless rejoinder.

Reyna stopped and waited for him to do the same. He seemed to draw an impatient breath.

'I suppose,' he snapped, 'that map came from Mr Harper?'

'Originally, yes.'

A strange silence followed. Then Thor Granville said,

'I think we'd better go to my house and talk this matter over. There seems to be many things that you're taking for granted.'

'Such as?' she challenged.

'For one thing, Miss Chapman, you will never be able to develop this island while I'm living on it.'

Reyna set her teeth.

'You can't prevent me doing just whatever I like with my half,' she told him stiffly.

'Can't I?' softly and yet with an unmistakable hint of authority in his voice. 'We shall see, Miss Chapman.'

The arrogance of the man! Reyna almost wished she had the money to develop—then knew she would not do it even if she had.

'We'll do as you say, Mr Granville, and talk!'

'This way.' He turned into a narrow, tree-shaded path which had been cut through the thick tropical vegetation. Half way along it was a clearing and Reyna glimpsed an oval-shaped swimming-pool complete with diving board and at one end, two changing-rooms. Thor Granville went on; the dog was nowhere to be seen, but Reyna heard the minah bird calling from somewhere in the trees.

'Hello! My name is Susan!'

'It's only a bird,' Thor said brusquely.

'I knew you had one.'

'Harper told you, of course.' Thor Granville strode on, throwing the words over his shoulder, the path being so narrow that Reyna was forced to walk behind him.

When at length she set eyes on the low white villa she could only gasp at its incredible beauty, and the fantastic setting of lawns and exotic flowers, of tall palms and flowering shrubs. There was a terraced rose garden; there were urns and statues and a picturesque fountain with the spray issuing from the mouths of three dolphins whose bodies were wreathed about one another. The water fell into a pool in which grew several aquatic plants, among which were giant water lilies whose flat, plate-like leaves measured a foot across.

'It's ... beautiful!' she breathed, not intending him to hear but realising that he *had* heard, because his expression changed. However, he merely said, in an abrupt, off-handed tone,

'We'll go round the back. It faces south, so it's cooler there.'

Of course, it would be cooler, she realised. The island was in the southern hemisphere, so one had to face south to be away from the Equator.

Every room on this north-facing side faced the sea—and so would those on the other side, mused Reyna, since the villa was built on the narrowest neck of the island. Thor Granville could walk from almost any room in his house on to the beach within minutes.

'It's been very well planned,' she commented, quite unable to hold back her appreciation. Her companion said nothing, but he did stop when she did, and waited for her to glance around.

One large window led on to a flower-draped patio, then came a velvet lawn which stretched down to the white sandy beach. Palms nodded everywhere, and delicate casuarinas fluttered in the breeze. Birds flitted about—the Seychelles sunbirds, a paradise flycatcher, and the conspicuous bulbul with its bright yellow-brown eyes, its black crest and orange bill. As they came round to the back of the villa Reyna's eye was caught by the brilliant red cardinals in the frangipani outside the verandah and she gave another involuntary gasp. Such unbelievable beauty! What right had a man so detestable as Thor Granville to be enjoying all these luxuries of nature? With all this in his possession, how could he have been so unkind to that poor old man?

She stopped again, quite unconsciously, to stare at the lagoon, its waters rippling gently as a breeze skimmed over its surface. As the breeze drifted inshore it whispered through the lofty foliage of the palms, like an echo of the

water caressing the shore. She gave a sigh and turned to
follow Thor Granville again, passing trees that she could
not name. Some she could name, however—the merantis,
and the junipers with their lovely rose-coloured perfumed
trunks. There was a mango with an exotic creeper on it, the
crimson flowers drooping in clusters like fuchsias.

'In here,' Thor Granville invited as they came to an
open window that led into a small apartment cooled by a
fan suspended from the ceiling. 'Sit down,' he said
brusquely. 'Perhaps you would like a drink?'

She hesitated, wishing she had brought up her rucksack
which contained a flask of coffee and a bottle of lemonade.

'I'd like a drink of water, please.'

He had been on his way to an antique cabinet which, she
realised, had been cleverly converted to a drinks cupboard,
but at her request he turned and to her surprise she saw
the thin lips curve in the merest hint of a smile. His eyes
too held amusement as he said,

'I don't think there's any need to carry your antagonism
quite that far, Miss Chapman.'

If it was his intention to disconcert her then he had the
satisfaction of knowing that he had succeeded. She
coloured, averting her head so as to hide her expression.

'I'll give you iced lemonade.' A statement, spoken in a
tone that brooked no argument. Reyna, although taking ex-
ception to it, made no comment, convinced as she was that
he would give her the lemonade no matter what she said.

She accepted the glass, which was delightfully cold to
her hand. She would have liked to put it to her lips at once,
and quench her thirst, but some perverse little streak made
her resist the temptation. She would not give him the
satisfaction of seeing her eagerness, so she placed the glass
on a small table at her elbow.

She glanced around, noticing the alabaster clock on a
buhl cabinet, a priceless Sèvres vase on a corner shelf, and
a silver-gilt candelabrum on a mahogany side table.

Thor Granville was a man of culture, obviously. Pity his manners were so contrary to his taste!

'Well, Miss Chapman,' he began when he himself was seated, 'perhaps we can discuss this business and come to an agreement.'

CHAPTER THREE

REYNA picked up her glass and took a drink. She was fast realising that she could be treading on slippery ground owing to the fact that she could not expand on the 'plans she had for development. It was amusing, really, when she came to think about it, because when she had totted up her assets a month ago she was a little alarmed to find that her bank balance was no more than a hundred and twenty pounds. She had been buying new carpets and refitting her little kitchen during the past few months and as a result she had not only failed to save from her monthly cheque but had drawn rather drastically on her reserves.

'You obviously object strongly to the idea of having tourists here,' she said, merely to open the conversation and to break a silence which seemed likely to stretch to some what awkward lengths.

'As I've said, Miss Chapman, there will be no development while I'm on this island.'

She seethed at his intolerable air of command. Yet she was curious as to his reason for not being interested in development. He knew he could not now get his hands on the other half of the island, so, if it were monetary gain he was after, then surely he would be ready to talk business.

'I fail to see, Mr Granville,' she said at length, 'how you can be so presumptuous as to act as though you owned the whole of the island ...' She let her words trail off as she noticed the strange, unfathomable expression that settled on his cold, unemotional features.

'My word is law here,' he returned. 'If I wanted development it would be done; as I don't want it, then you can put all ideas of building hotels right out of your mind.' As he spoke his eyes were on the liquid in his glass, but they darted towards Reyna in a calculating glance that—for no reason at all—served as a reminder of her bank balance. She'd always had a sense of humour, passed on from her aunt, she supposed, and now she found amusement taking the place of her anger. 'Something amuses you, Miss Chapman?' The very tone savoured of a stricture—as if he were telling her that laughter was forbidden, even secret laughter. But his question was bypassed as the full force of his previous remark hit her. It set her temper aflame, bringing sparks to her eyes.

'Mr Granville,' she flashed back at him haughtily, 'if I decide to build hotels on my half of this island, then neither you nor anyone else will stop me!'

'So the gloves are off,' he observed without hesitation.

'They were off the moment I received your insolent letter! In any case, I'd heard from poor Mr Harper just how cruelly you'd been treating him!'

He appeared to be totally unaffected by this, ignoring it as he said,

'The best thing you can do, Miss Chapman, is sell your share to me. I'm willing to offer you a fair price——'

'I'm not prepared to sell,' she broke in, seeing no gain in allowing him to continue. Even had she wanted to sell she could not do so, for although she had made no specific promise to Patch, she was obligated by the knowledge that his sole reason for giving her half the island was so that this arrogant, high-handed creature sitting here could not get his greedy hands on it.

'You haven't considered the advantages,' he said. 'Half an island's no good at all to you.'

'I'm quite happy with it, Mr Granville.'

Reyna picked up her glass again and took a drink. It was delicious, and she wondered if he grew his own lemons or if he had them brought in on the supply boat. Where did he get his water? she was suddenly asking herself, then thought there were probably streams on the island. She was eager to go out there and explore and decided to bring this conversation to an end.

'I feel we have nothing really important to discuss, Mr Granville, so I'll leave you. There's just one thing: there's a cemetery on the island——' She opened out the map which she had taken from her handbag and spread it on the floor in front of her. 'The solicitor told me it was a private cemetery. Is that right?'

'Yes, it is.' He looked faintly puzzled, his eyes falling lazily to the map, which was a very old one—the original of which he had a copy.

'I would like you to show me this cemetery, just to give me a landmark as a starting point for my search.'

'Search?' he repeated swiftly.

'Oh, not for the treasure, Mr Granville. I'll leave you to do that,' she could not help adding, just to be spiteful. 'You've been digging, so Mr Harper told me, so I wouldn't like to intrude on what must be a most pleasurable pastime. I was merely saying that I'd be searching for the border between your land and mine.' She was not enjoying herself as much as she had anticipated when she had sent off that letter and at the same time made up her mind to come here and 'plague' the man, as Patch had wanted her to. For one thing, Thor Granville was by no means put out by her suggestions regarding probable development, and for another, there was something—some indefinable tinge of uneasiness in her mind which she could not understand.

However, her reference to the treasure and to his having been digging for it did appear to have enraged him, for she had the satisfaction of seeing the first traces of that devilish temper which Patch had mentioned. Little threads of crimson colour had crept beneath the tan of his skin; those eyebrows had come together in a frown and those steely glints in his eyes were suddenly like sparks of hot metal.

'Be careful, Miss Chapman,' he warned in a low and

almost guttural tone of voice. 'You might find yourself in a most uncomfortable and humiliating position if you fail to treat me with respect again.'

'What are you threatening me with?' she wanted to know, fully aware that her show of bravery was only a veneer. She was tingling a little, with a sudden fear. After all, she was alone on this island with him, and the boat would not be here for another five hours. It behoved her to be careful, much as it went against the grain. To her surprise he laughed.

'Not what you think, Miss Chapman. If I'm not mistaken your good friend Mr Harper will have told you that I have no time at all for women.'

'He did,' she returned briefly, her colour rising painfully at his first sentence. But there was something much more forthright to come.

'In that case, you'll have nothing to fear as regards the kind of assault you had in mind just now.' He was laughing at her embarrassment, thoroughly enjoying her discomfiture. Fury rose suffocating in her throat, causing her to stumble over her words.

'You're—detestable! You—you haven't a sp-spark of delicacy in you!'

The lazy topaz eyes flickered over her contemptuously.

'Go and find your demarcation line, Miss Chapman,' he advised. 'The exercise will serve to calm your nerves. I was going to say it would help to cool your temper, but by the time you've walked round this island you'll be ready for a dip in the sea. You've chosen the hottest part of the day for your task. Let me see the map.' But he was already telling her where to find the cemetery, and he used the map merely to give her the starting point.

'Thank you,' she said stiffly, turning to the wide window through which she had entered the lovely room.

'Don't mention it,' he returned, lifting a long brown hand to suppress a yawn.

Reyna was fuming with temper, hot with embarrassment, and troubled by something she could not understand. The island was beautiful, but she was half wishing she had never seen it. She had been far too optimistic in her assumption that she could successfully cross swords with the formidable Thor Granville. His cool hauteur, his imperious, domineering manner, his contempt of her sex — all these had been too much for her. If only she had his sort of temperament she might have had more chance of holding her own—although she very much doubted it. As it was, with her more fiery nature, she had suffered a crushing defeat. Yes, might as well admit it, mortifying though it was.

She hurried off, anxious to put some distance between him and her. Was he watching from the window? It was difficult not to turn around, but she forced herself to go on. Soon the tropical vegetation was hiding her from his view and she felt better. But she was angry that her first impression of the island was spoiled. She had imagined wandering about, exploring the coral coves, finding that old Creole house that was now in ruins but where the young couple had lived. The solicitor had given her an ancient document along with the deeds, a document that covered the whole of the island. She had discovered, on reading this document, that the couple in question had been a carpenter aged seventeen, and a seamstress aged sixteen. They had married and for a wedding present had been given the half of Surcoufe now owned by Thor Granville. It was a romantic story, appealing to Reyna's imagination. A couple in their teens, just married, and coming here, to this paradise island in the sun. How happy they must have been!

It was an interesting history even without the ghosts — the 'nams', as they were called in the Seychelles—who were supposed to come out on the march from the pirate cemetery at midnight, so it was reported in the ancient document.

Reyna found the cemetery, itself almost buried in a tangled mass of undergrowth. But she managed to move around it, fascinated as she discovered several flat stones that had been roughly laid down as gravestones.

So deeply absorbed was she that on hearing a harsh, gruff, 'Hark! Hark! Hark!' she let out a little cry of fright and the map fluttered from her hand.

'Oh ... you silly thing!' She was not sure whether she meant herself or the bright green parakeet which was perched inquisitively on the branch of a tamarind tree a few yards from where she stood. She glanced at her watch, realised she had wasted too much time already, and set off in the direction indicated by Thor Granville. She soon saw that the border line moved about in so haphazard a manner that, as Patch had said, it would be difficult to develop one half of Surcoufe without touching the other. Well, it wasn't important. As far as she was concerned there would be no problems at all. She wandered on, intrigued by the different species of trees and flowers. She stopped often, to wonder at the aerial roots of a massive banyan or the delicate feathery foliage of a red sandalwood tree. She came unexpectedly upon a lovely arboreal climbing orchid with long sword-like leaves and pale green and pearl-white flowers, which had the delectable perfume of gardenias. Her wanderings brought her to the coast several times, and here she gazed with wonderment at the leaning takamaka trees which seemed designed to provide shade for the sandy beaches. The palms were numerous, as were the casuarinas. The hibiscus of the coast were smaller than those Reyna had seen in Thor Granville's garden, but one species, she noticed, had large golden flowers shaped like cups.

Still she wandered on, unaffected by the heat, and not even feeling hungry, so absorbing was her walk. Eventually, though, she did sit down and, taking the lemonade from her rucksack, poured some into the plastic beaker

she had brought with her, and drank thirstily. Her mind
was more than a little confused regarding the demarcation
line between the two halves of the island. In any case, there
was no means of separating the two from what she could
see. A bubbling stream tumbling down from a small rise
seemed to be the dividing line for some distance, but then
it twisted and turned as it met hard bands of coral lime-
stone in its bed and allowed its course to be diverted all
over the place. Short of erecting something man-made
there was no way of being able to say for sure that this
land was hers, or that Thor Granville's. It was not difficult
to see how he had come to consider the whole island to be
his, or how that couple had built their house on the wrong
land.

It suddenly came to Reyna that she ought to be making
her way back, as it was a quarter to three and she had
come a long way—in fact, she had an idea that she was
now on the opposite side of the island to where she wanted
to be. Should she cut round the coast or through the
middle? Through the middle, she decided; it would be
the shorter way. The vegetation was thick, but Thor Granville had kept the paths in good order—paths which, she
surmised, had originally been made by others who had
lived on Surcoufe.

Reyna's romantic mind brought in a vision of that young
couple again. Sixteen and seventeen ... Two children playing at love in this garden of Eden. A whole exotic island
to themselves, as no one else lived here at that time. They
must have wandered hand in hand among the tall trees
and cascading greenery, inhaling the musty hothouse
fragrance just as she was doing now, perhaps thinking, as
she was thinking, that here one could become lost in the
deep shadows of time, for the whole atmosphere evoked
the sensation of being in at the primeval, mysterious
creation of the world.

So engrossed was she in these most pleasant mind-wanderings that she failed to note the landmarks which she had originally picked out on the map. She had passed the House of Dogs, then a little shrine, overgrown for the most part but with a rusty crucifix poking through the prickly pears that had grown up around the shrine. She had missed these, and also the lovely carpet of pearly-white begonias which she had noticed in a shady under wood. Where was she, then? A map was useless if she did not know at what particular point she was standing now. A trifle worried, she debated on whether she should try to get to the coast road. Surcoufe was only one and a half miles across at its widest part, but it was two miles long, which meant that if she happened to proceed in the wrong direction she could find herself a fair distance from the place where she was to get the boat. She ought to be able to tell by the sun which way she must go, but unfortun-ately the sun was gradually becoming lower in the sky, and also the heavy cover of tropical vegetation was cutting out the sunlight. That was why it was so dim ... Or was the sun beginning to go down?

The sun shouldn't be going down yet! Here, so close to the Equator, the hours of night and day were about equal, so it should be totally dark at around six o'clock. Reyna looked at her watch and gave a little gasp. A quarter to four! She began to run, and to call out, thinking that if Thor Granville replied then she would have a direction to follow. But the closeness of the vegetation prevented her voice from carrying. If only she could find her way out of this dim part of the forest! She kept on running, aware that she might be proceeding in the wrong direction alto gether. She fell twice, having caught her foot in tangled roots of the trees. Her rucksack was becoming uncomfort ably heavy and perspiration was pouring from her fore-head and trickling down her face. Why on earth her mind had wandered off into that dreamy state she did not know Also, she ought to have taken more care to watch the time

The guide on the boat had warned her that if she were not punctual they would have to go without her. The warning had not troubled Reyna overmuch, since she was confident of being there on time. But of course she had reckoned on having a conducted tour, and that Thor Granville would ensure her being in plenty of time to catch the boat. If only she hadn't been so independent this would never have happened, she thought as she ran along, wishing she could find the path which she had somehow lost. She called again, but with no more success than before. It was now four o'clock and she despaired of catching the boat that day. A night on this island ... with the formidable Thor Granville! Still, it could have been worse, she thought, trying not to let the mishap trouble her too much. Thor Granville could—in addition to all his other vices— have been the kind of man with whom no woman was safe. By his own admission she had nothing to fear and, thankfully, she knew she could believe him.

She would be invited to stay in that lovely villa, which would be a pleasant experience, she supposed. What time would she get a boat tomorrow? Thor Granville would know, of course.

It was a quarter past five when she arrived back at the place where she had first come face to face with Thor Granville. He was nowhere to be seen, nor was the dog. Reyna made her way to the back door of the villa and knocked; she was kept waiting so long that she began to wonder if the owner was out looking for her. But at last he came, Shah at his side. He had changed into white slacks and a light, pearl-grey shirt which seemed, somehow, to accentuate the steely glints in his lazy topaz eyes. She looked up into a cold, arrogant countenance and said in a low voice,

'Has the boat gone without me?' It was a stupid question; Reyna realised this even before his caustic reply was voiced.

'Well, it hasn't taken you on board, has it?'

She coloured hotly, hating him with a black venom. Why was he looking so immaculate anyway! He made her feel like a tramp, standing here with her face dusty, and damp with perspiration. Her jeans had suffered from her tumbles, since the ground had been wet beneath the trees, and even her hands were not too clean, since she had been poking around those gravestones.

'I shall have to stay the night, then.' She tried to inject some modicum of dignity into her voice, but was at the same time painfully conscious of the fact that she was asking him for accommodation. Her glance strayed; she estimated by the size of the villa that there must be at least three bedrooms. Three? Odd, surely, that he should have had so many included in the house. Perhaps he was not such a recluse after all; perhaps he entertained visitors now and then.

'*The* night?' he repeated, his emphasis puzzling her.

She moistened her lips. Darn the man for being so tall! She hated having to tilt her head right back like this!

'Yes,' she muttered. 'I suppose you can ...' Her voice trailed off to silence. The suggestion that she sleep at his house should come from him, and she waited, a stiff 'thank you' ready on her lips.

The angular mask of his face never moved as he said. 'What was the idea, missing the boat like that?'

'The——!' She stared up at him, her eyes blank and startled. 'What do you mean?' she demanded. 'You're not suggesting I missed it deliberately?'

'That, Miss Chapman, is exactly what I am suggesting.' So cool, so emphatic his assertion. Reyna set her teeth, anger rising at his accusation.

'And why, Mr Granville, do you suppose I would want to spend a night on Surcoufe?'

'In order to annoy me,' came the suave reply.

She felt her anger increasing to fury.

'So my presence will annoy you? You appear to have forgotten, Mr Granville, that half of this island belongs to me. Am I not allowed to occupy my own property if I wish?'

A strange unfathomable silence followed and once again Reyna was affected by that tinge of uneasiness which she had experienced before. But all she heard Thor Granville say was,

'I'll show you to your quarters, Miss Chapman. Come this way.'

To her surprise he came out of the house and turned abruptly towards the narrow path which had been cut through the jungle-like vegetation, the path along which she had been led when first visiting the villa. She herself just now had approached by another path which ran between exotic flower borders from where drifted the heady perfumes which she was soon to associate with Surcoufe alone.

She followed him along the path, automatically glancing at the clearing where the pool was, and now she noticed a fountain close by, its water blue-grey in the mystic glow from the lowering sun. But her mind was not on pools and fountains, or even the rare beauty of the scene around her as she walked briskly behind the tall, angular figure whose pace was causing her to skip now and then so as not to allow the distance between them to stretch too far. She was dwelling on the word 'quarters' and was by now apprehensively aware that she was not to sleep in the villa, nor even in its vicinity.

Thor Granville was now leading her out of his own grounds; he strode on for another few minutes and then stopped.

'There.' He pointed, to a small log cabin which was almost hidden from view. 'That, Miss Chapman, happens to be on your property. You will no doubt be happy to occupy it for your fortnight's stay here.'

'Fortnight!' she gasped. There mustn't be a boat, then. 'I can't live in *that* for a fortnight!'

'What do you expect, the Dorchester?' he sneered.

'Is there no boat that will be calling here in less than a fortnight?' she asked, managing to hide the choking fury that had resulted from his sarcasm.

The lazy eyes roved her face contemptuously.

'You know there won't be a boat, Miss Chapman,' he replied and, turning on his heel, he strode away and was soon lost to view among the trees and bushes. Reyna stood, aware of her heart thumping against her ribs. The sun was falling with speed now and mysterious shadows were gathering all around her. She swallowed saliva collecting on her tongue, but no amount of swallowing would move the little ball of fear that had risen in her throat. Was ever a man so vile as Thor Granville! Even with his intense dislike of women he could at least have put her up for the night—— But it was not for one night only, he had said. She had been told that the supply boat called once a fortnight only, so unless that hateful man was telling a lie in an attempt to frighten her, the supply boat must have called at the island either very early this morning or yesterday. A fortnight. Surely he could get in touch with Mahé. How would he go on if he were ill——? Again her thoughts cut; by no stretch of imagination could she see that hardy vigorous Thor Granville requiring the ministrations of a doctor.

At last she turned, to stare at the log cabin. At this point or thereabouts it would seem there was part of the boundary, but it was a part which Reyna had bypassed because she wanted to cover as much ground as possible before it was time to return to the beach. She glanced up, to the mauve-grey sky of early evening. Then, realising that it would soon be dark, she went over to the door of the cabin and pushed it inwards. No lock, or even a fastening of any kind whatsoever. Meeting her eyes in the dimness of the cabin were a truckle bed which to her surprise seemed to offer some reasonable degree of comfort, a rattan chair and a table that appeared to have been a garden table at one time, as its wooden top was bleached and badly split. On a shelf was a tall jug and a bowl. Reyna's eyes glittered. The jug held water—she knew it instinctively. And the truckle bed ... it had been put up within the last hour or so! The blanket, though grey in colour rather like the old army blankets, was clean to her touch as she bent to finger it. She turned it down, to find a pillow with a snow-white slip on it. There was another blanket covering the canvas of the bed, and that was all.

'So he got this ready as soon as it dawned on him that I'd missed the boat!' Reyna felt in this moment of fury that she would have done him an injury had it been at all possible. Hateful, insufferable creature! She thought of the comfort the lovely white villa would have offered, and frowned at the truckle bed; she imagined the meal which Thor Granville was probably even now preparing for himself, and thought of the sandwiches she had put in her rucksack; they would be dry and unappetising by now, she concluded. However, she ate them, sitting on the chair and feeling exceedingly sorry for herself. She recalled that last day before school broke up for the six weeks' summer vacation. Janie had said enviously,

'Holidaying in the Seychelles! You lucky blighter, Reyna!' And the other teachers, too, had added their comments. Of course, none of them knew she was visiting Surcoufe; they presumed she would be staying all the time at the hotel she had mentioned. 'Sounds luxurious by the description you've given us,' said Janie. 'Private bath and French cuisine!'

Luxurious! A log cabin planted in the middle of a forest, with no running water, even!

Reyna slept in her clothes, too scared to undress. In any

case, she had no nightgown with her. Nightgown! Her dainty frills and flounces in a bed like this!

She tossed and turned for a while, wishing she had a candle or a torch. She wanted a drink and all her coffee had gone, and most of the lemonade too. She supposed the water was all right for drinking, as otherwise it would not be there—unless it was for washing only, she thought. No, surely even a man like Thor Granville would have provided her with drinking water. He hadn't provided her with a glass, though, but he probably guessed she had some kind of a drinking vessel in her rucksack, which of course she did have.

She slept fitfully and awoke to the sun filtering through the numerous cracks in the cabin walls. Slipping from beneath the blanket, she stretched luxuriously. She felt fine! She would feel even better after a wash and change of clothing. It had been suffocatingly hot in that bed, what with her cotton jeans and blouse, and that blanket as well. She had several times been about to throw off the blanket, but she was afraid of something crawling over her in the darkness. It would have been the supreme humiliation to give that insufferable man the satisfaction of hearing her scream out in the middle of the night.

She washed her face and hands, then the rest of her body. Clean underwear felt delightfully fresh after she had had worn those clothes for twenty-four hours. The shorts were very short, but as Thor Granville was immune to the attractions of the female anatomy she felt quite safe. She was glad she had brought such things as a brush and comb, a blusher and lipstick. She even had a tiny bottle of perfume, a present from her aunt before she left for her holiday.

'Hmm . . .' she breathed with satisfaction. 'I look fresh and I smell nice! I'm ready for that despicable man—more than ready!' She put the small mirror she had been using on to the shelf, propping it against the water jug. Then she stepped back, endeavouring to see a little more of herself. Earlier, she had opened the door wide in order to get some light, as there were no windows in the cabin. The mirror faced the door and with the light on it she could obtain a fairly good view—at least as far as her waist. 'You'll be expecting to see me looking as I was last evening—dressed in those grubby jeans and that blouse that had gone all limp. Well, Mr arrogant, pompous, self-opinionated, superior Thor Granville, you're in for a surprise! I'm more than ready . . .' Her voice tailed off in a sort of gurgle at the back of her throat as she spun around. Thor Granville was standing there, about a couple of feet from the door, his lazy topaz eyes unmoving as they watched the colour flood into her cheeks.

'Oh . . . !' Why didn't the floor open up and take her mercifully out of this man's sight! Never in her wildest dreams could she have imagined herself to be in such an embarrassing position as this. She could neither move nor speak; she was distressingly conscious of her colour still rising, of her lower lip caught tightly between her teeth and, worst of all, she was profoundly alive to the fact that those steely glints were now displaying contempt alongside the hint of sardonic amusement that had crept into Thor Granville's eyes, eyes that swept over her body from head to toe.

'Good morning, Miss Chapman,' he greeted her at last. 'I trust you slept well?'

She gulped down whatever it was that blocked her throat. 'Fine—thank you, Mr Granville.'

A momentary pause and then, slowly and—surprisingly —with a hint of amusement,

'You do appear to be in fine fettle, Miss Chapman. That string of adjectives was not at all bad for this time of the morning.' Again his eyes took in her appearance.

She turned away, furious that her confidence of a

moment ago had been shattered by the untimely appearance of the man she detested more than anyone she had ever known in the whole of her life.

'If I apologised, Mr Granville,' she managed, 'I would be insincere.'

'I admire you for your honesty, Miss Chapman.'

'Admire?' She swung around again, her eyes seeking his. 'You amaze me,' she said.

'For what reason?' His glance strayed to Shah, sitting on his haunches, quietly looking at Reyna. She wondered how Thor Granville came to be here, then thought that perhaps he was out walking with the dog and had decided to walk past the cabin just to make sure she was all right. He would not have expected to hear her talking to herself, so she could hardly blame him for overhearing what she was saying about him.

'What reason?' His question was repeated automatically as with a back-switch of memory she was recalling what Patch had told her about this man's opinion of women. 'Well, you dislike my sex, don't you?'

'The fact that I have little or no time for your sex does not preclude my admiring your particular honesty, Miss Chapman.'

'Must I feel complimented?' she inquired tartly.

'I never pay a woman compliments. I was merely making a statement, Miss Chapman.' He drew a small package from his pocket as he spoke. 'I remembered last night that I hadn't provided you with soap. Obviously you have some, but you might as well have this.' He held it out and she took it, noticing the long slender fingers, fingers, she thought, that could be cruel ... never kind, and caressing and comforting ...

Now why on earth had a thought like that come into her head? she was asking herself a moment later as she watched his tall figure disappearing into the forest.

CHAPTER FOUR

HE had not asked her if she wanted breakfast, and she went from the cabin wondering if he were intending to let her starve. Not that she could, of course, with all this fruit about, but she did think longingly of such things as bacon and eggs and toast and marmalade. A cup of steaming, milky coffee would not come amiss either.

She had noticed some wild pineapples yesterday and she decided that one or two of those would suffice for her breakfast. But she would need a knife. Oh, well, she would find some other fruit ... She had wandered on to the wooded region backing on to the beach and now she saw the dog race ahead of her, then stop, waiting for his master. She turned, wishing with all her heart that she could ignore the man, but instead she asked him for the loan of a knife.

'A knife? What for?'

'I'll need one if I'm to live on fruit,' she said.

Did those thin lips twitch? she wondered, staring up into his angular, saturnine features.

'Come with me and I'll get you one,' he said brusquely.

So it hadn't worked. Reyna gritted her teeth, as angry with herself as with him. He had guessed at once that what she was really asking for was some breakfast. She would starve before she'd hint at anything like that again!

'Have I really to wait a fortnight before I can get off this island?' she asked, standing at the door where he had left her to go into his immaculate kitchen and bring her a knife.

'Why, are you tired of it already?' He handed her the knife.

She ignored the sarcasm of that and said,

'I am naturally inconvenienced by my lack of clothing, and other things, too.'

She was uncomfortable, standing there at the open door, the knife in her hand. She had come here to 'plague' him, she recalled, to throw out numerous threats about developing the half of Surcoufe which belonged to her. Instead, it was Thor Granville who was plaguing her, really—or perhaps 'subtle torture' would be a better definition of his treatment of her.

'You appear to have a change of clothing,' he observed, his lazy eyes flickering over her in a cursory glance.

'One change? I need more than that!'

'You're staying in Victoria, I think you said—or was it in one of the hotels on Beau Vallon Beach?'

She told him the name of the hotel, realising bleakly that, since she had booked one of the detached bungalows, she would not be missed, simply because she had dispensed with the room service in order to save money.

'Very different from your cosy little cabin over there,' Thor Granville was commenting heartlessly.

Reyna's chin lifted.

'I was comfortable enough, Mr Granville!'

'Perhaps I ought not to have supplied you with the bed. Had you been forced to sleep on the floor you wouldn't be feeling so ready to do battle with me this morning. It *was* that which you were about to say when I so inconveniently intruded on your pleasant, one-sided conversation?'

She glared at him, but said,

'Yes, it was! And I'd be ready even if I'd slept on the floor! You can remove your truckle bed just whenever you like!'

'I might just do that,' he threatened, and she knew by his expression that he was making no idle threat.

'I asked if it were possible for me to leave here before a fortnight,' she snapped.

'No, it isn't. The supply boat came yesterday morning and won't be here for two weeks—or, to be exact, thirteen days.'

She glanced at him with suspicion.

'Do you mean to say that you couldn't get into touch with the capital no matter how urgent the matter might be?'

To her surprise he made no answer to this, merely saying that if she wanted drinking water then she could help herself from his tap over the sink. If she wanted to wash her clothes, however, she could do this in the stream, as the women on Mahé and the other islands did.

'You'll have seen the laundry drying on the ground—or perhaps you haven't been in Mahé long enough for that?'

'I arrived the day before yesterday.'

'Ah ... and couldn't wait to get here and threaten me with these development plans you've had in mind.' He paused a moment. 'I'm still willing to buy your half, Miss Chapman.'

'No doubt you are,' she returned shortly, 'but you didn't manage to exploit Mr Harper and you'll not manage to exploit me. Do you think I don't know why you're so anxious to get the whole island into your hands?'

He gave an impatient exclamation and turned from her, closing the door in her face as he went into the house.

Reyna stood a moment, fury surging through her whole body. The rude, ill-mannered opinionated male creature

She turned away from his door, looking at the knife in her hand. She'd a good mind to return it to him—through the air! Of course, though, he was wild because she refused to sell; that was the reason for his manner with her She suspected that he was in as great a fury as she, but he had the gift of hiding his real feelings beneath a veneer of arrogant composure. If only she could do the same she wouldn't find herself being humiliated every time she encountered him.

Try to forget him, she advised herself. If she found something to occupy her mind then she might be able to do so. The first thing, though, was to have that fruit. It proved to be delicious, and her thirst had been quenched as well. The next thing was to wash her clothes in the stream, and after that she made her bed, wondering if, later in the day, she would find it had been taken away. Let him take it! She could rough it here for a fortnight.

The old Creole house marked on the map stood lost in a tangle of tree ferns, lemon grass, wild vanilla and other vegetation that had run wild over many years. Reyna, having found the house after searching about in the vicinity of the place marked on the map, stood enthralled, seeing those two children living here, coming to it on their honeymoon from their homes on the island of Mahé. How had they built it? Had they done it themselves? Who had given them half of Surcoufe? Of their parents nothing was known, according to the old document which Reyna had in her possession. Were they orphans, then? What a pity that deeds had not come into being before they did. It was not known from whom this young couple had received this handsome gift.

After standing there for a long while, it was with a mingling of awe and reverence that Reyna approached the Creole villa. She suddenly felt saddened by the sight. It must have known such happiness ... but now it stood forlorn and lonely, its roof half torn away—probably by one of the fierce winds that occasionally struck these islands. She could not tell if its windows were all smashed, owing to the green drapery covering the walls, but she concluded that they were. It was a happy surprise, therefore, when she discovered on dragging away a rather obstinate creeper that this one window at least was intact, and the door, although sitting askew owing to the disintegration of the hinges, seemed to be in a reasonably good state of preservation.

She dragged off more of the clinging vines and creepers. It was a pleasant, tender occupation, this task of bringing to light the villa again. And as she worked in the sunshine, with the breeze from the sea bringing in a white drift of cloud to billow in the sky, Reyna could not think of anything but this couple, whose names were Melidor and Julie. Did they have children? No children were mentioned in the document, and at the turn of the century the couple had sold their half of the island to a Frenchman who had never lived here. It was only about seventy years since, aware they were growing old, Melidor and his wife had sold out and left Surcoufe for ever. Was it a reluctant decision? Or did they look forward to ending their days in a more civilised world? Reyna thought not; she wanted to think that the couple left with tears in their eyes, since it was more romantic that way. Yes, she admitted, ruefully flicking a tear from her own eye, she was a romantic—always had been and always would be—though anyone seeing her with Thor Granville would find that hard to believe. With him she desired only to be shrewish and quarrelsome   just to match his own nasty personality. Well, if not to match it exactly, to combat it, then. Not that she was holding her own very well, she reflected, wishing even yet again that she could assume an air of cold hauteur and contempt which would rile him as she was riled by his.

She had sat down for a rest, and her pensive eyes were glancing around at the interfusion of creepers and shrubs, of vines and herbs and grasses. Then unexpectedly her roving eye caught a drift of colour—rose-purple—among the grasses on the far side of the villa.

'Periwinkle!' she exclaimed. 'It must have been here when they were living in the house!' Of course, it might not have been, but Reyna was quite prepared to believe it had. This discovery led to further exploration of what had once been the garden and to her delight she discovered several bushes and other flowering plants. 'I've found a treasure!' she cried aloud. 'Not *the* treasure—but one much more valuable—although that greedy avaricious Thor Granville wouldn't agree——' She broke off abruptly, remembering how he had overheard her earlier on. She had no intention of him overhearing her again; she had no intention of even telling him she had discovered a treasure. It was her secret, and this was her house. Yes, the old Creole villa was on her deeds, not his! Let him have everything else, but this was hers alone.

She dreamed on as she began to drag at the weeds which were strangling a lovely hibiscus bush. How had it survived all these years? Now, it could have some light, some warm sunshine to make it thrive as it did when Julie planted it as a tiny sprig. It would be Julie, Reyna decided; Melidor would be busy with such things as those orange trees over there in what looked very much like an orchard, and he would have planted that pomegranate tree, and that little thicket of bananas. She had only just noticed the orchard, for every tree seemed to be supporting a parasite of some kind, and it was only by sheer good fortune that she had noticed the brilliant crimson flowers of the pomegranate tree and from there her eager, wandering gaze had picked up the other trees. She thought suddenly: these can't really be the plants put in by Julie and Melidor—but they're definitely from the *seeds* of those plants. She found date palms, of course, because these were growing elsewhere as well, and a jackfruit alongside a golden apple tree. Excitement throbbed through her veins, and yet it was a sort of uncomplicated excitement, as if the discoveries were ordained ... as if all this had lain here, quietly and dreamily, waiting for *her* to come and set it to rights ...

Set it to rights? Was that her intention? She had a mere fortnight. A great deal could be done in two weeks, especially as she had nothing else to interfere with her work. Besides, she could come back and stay for another month.

She had six weeks' holiday in all ... She came to a decision
almost immediately. She would return to the hotel in two
weeks' time, pay her bill, collect her belongings, and come
back to Surcoufe.

It was dusk when eventually she returned to the cabin,
having made a meal of the orange-coloured bananas whose
pulp was more delicious than those which she got at home.
She had been a little hesitant at first on seeing the unfamiliar colour of the pulp, but one sample of the delicate
flavour convinced her that there was no danger in eating
them. She had brought some water with her, from the jug
which Thor Granville had given her, but she felt hungry
and thirsty again now and although she had brought some
fruit with her to the cabin, she longed for a nice juicy
steak or a rainbow trout smothered in almonds.

For the next two days she saw nothing of Thor Granville,
even though she called at his villa each morning to fill her
jug with drinking water. Either he was deliberately keeping out of her way or he was busy on some task of his own.
Reyna had begun to let her thoughts return to him, and
found herself puzzled that a man of such vigour and in-
telligence should be living here, all alone, with the dog and
the minah bird. She had never seen the cat and felt sure
that it must have died since Patch was here. The tortoises
could be anywhere, since the grounds of the Villa Surcoufe
were extensive.

The Creole house had been thoroughly explored and to
Reyna's delight she found that it had appeared much more
dilapidated than it really was. On the deeds it was a house;
in the old document it was a Creole villa, but according to
the solicitors at Rye it was considered to be a ruin. It had
certainly had the appearance of a ruin at first glance, with
its roof half gone like that and its walls practically buried
by wild vegetation and young trees that had grown up from
seeds scattered by the wind. Reyna had great difficulty with

these trees, some of which were saplings, but others were now well established and would require implements for their removal. Sometimes, as she considered the task she had set herself, Reyna would wonder if it was an impossible one. But she had rarely allowed anything to beat her, and the more she thought about that young couple, the more she wanted to put their little house in order.

She had started on the garden, then left it to go inside the house and begin clearing away the grass and vines that were growing up through the floorboards. And as she worked, and saw something for that work, she became so enthusiastic that she was already furnishing it, determining to find pieces that would go with the wooden ceiling and walls, to find the kind of rugs that would look just right on the floor once it was polished, and had the holes repaired, of course.

It would never be a luxury villa, but Reyna had no desire that it should be. Her imagination, and her flair for grouping together things that harmonised, would ensure her complete satisfaction with the end product of her labours.

There had been a verandah all around the house, but part of this was missing, appearing to have rotted away along with the part of the roof that had come down. With the rest of the house, it had been a most fortunate circumstance that the vegetation—and more especially a creeper with large glossy leaves—had served as a protection for the wood of which the villa was made. Rain had run off those large leaves on to the ground, and the walls were left comparatively dry. Inevitably there were rotting timbers here and there, but Reyna estimated that these could be replaced at a price which she could afford if she saved as much as possible every month from her pay. In a year this could be a charming villa to which she and her aunt could come every summer. Yes, Reyna had it all planned, and she could see Thor Granville gnashing his teeth every time she visited the island.

Meanwhile, Reyna had no doubt that she could make one half of the villa habitable while she was here, and she hoped that, when she went back to Mahé in ten days' time, she would be able to find someone who would come over at least once a month, just to see that the garden didn't become overgrown again.

She worked until the sun was going down and then went back to the cabin, making sure that she was not seen by the man whom she had come to regard as her enemy. He had never even come to see if she was all right—not since that first morning when he had heard her talking to herself about him. Reyna still went hot whenever she thought about it, and was heartily glad that she was not coming into daily contact with him. The Creole villa was effectively hidden by tropical vegetation which had been running wild for years and even the path that had once existed and which led from the villa to a lovely coral cove marked Pirates' Bay on the map was totally obliterated. So she had no anxieties about Thor Granville's discovering her activities. Also, the villa was at the opposite end of the island from his and in distance about three-quarters of a mile away.

It was when she was coming back to the cabin on the third day that she encountered Thor Granville again. She had chosen the coast road and was enjoying the breeze on her face and the delicate drift of scents that came from the wild flowers growing almost down to the shoreline, when to her amazement she saw Shah jumping up and down in the water. She stopped, too intrigued by his activities even to look at the man striding along, his lean supple frame swinging wih the easy gait of an athlete. The dog was actually chasing fish! They jumped out of the water to escape him, while he jumped after them in a series of hops rather like those of a frog but much quicker.

'Well!' exclaimed Reyna audibly. 'Am I seeing things?'

'Have you never seen a dog fishing before, Miss Chapman?'

She turned her head, her eyes bewildered as her thoughts remained on the activities of the dog.

'No, I haven't. It's incredible—just look at him!' she cried in excitement as, her attention having instantly returned to the dog, she saw him miss catching a fish by inches. 'Does he ever get them?'

'Sometimes.'

'You'd think they'd have the sense to go down instead of jumping up out of the water like that.'

'Do fish have sense?' he said sarcastically. 'I wouldn't have thought so.'

'There's no need for sarcasm,' she bristled, angry with herself for forgetting her antagonism in the excitement of watching the dog.

He looked her over, from her sandals to her shorts, then to her blouse. Acutely aware that they were by no means clean even though they had certainly been clean when she set out from the cabin that morning at a quarter past six, Reyna found herself holding her breath. The man was no fool; it was no use pretending he would be blind to the fact that she had been doing some kind of manual work. It was sheer bad luck that she had encountered him now, when she had managed to escape a meeting for the past two evenings. She had no idea why it should seem important that he should remain in ignorance of her activities at the villa, but it did seem important and she was wondering how she could answer him if he decided to question her. He merely said, in an expressionless voice,

'You're not finding life too boring here?'

Was it imagination, or was he hoping to hear that she *was* finding life boring? She answered lightly,

'Not at all, Mr Granville.'

'You don't mind the isolation?'

'It would be all the same if I did,' she could not help retorting. As a matter of fact she was thoroughly enjoying it, apart from the discomforts of her accommodation and the

monotony of her diet. After the hectic two weeks at the end
of term when there had been exams and the consequent
marking of papers, prize-giving and sports days, the clearing out of desks and stripping the classroom in readiness
for the decorators, it was heavenly to have a period of peace
and quietness like this.

'What do you imply by that?' Thor Granville wanted to
know. 'If you came here expecting me to entertain you then
you were obviously in for a disappointment.'

Reyna sent him a scornful glance.

'You couldn't be civil if you tried, could you?'

The topaz eyes glinted.

'Could you?' he countered softly.

She looked away, to watch the dog again, trying to keep
her temper in check. Keep cool, she was telling herself.
You'll hold your own a little better then. She continued to
watch Shah, who was moving out, towards the reef, and a
large fish was leaping out of the water and swerving this
way and that in an effort to escape those vicious fangs.
Thor Granville moved and she looked at him, wondering
why he was here with her, and not, as she would have expected, walking away towards his house.

'I can scarcely treat you with civility,' she said at length,
'while you're so intent on being uncivil to me, Mr Granville.'

'You ask for it,' he stated. 'I'm at a loss to comprehend
what your motives are in coming here and threatening to
build hotels and high-rise holiday flats and the rest.'

'And why should you be so concerned? I'm not going to
encroach on your land.' She felt guilty and specious, pretending like this, but as he deserved it she could not resist
adding, 'It will of course interfere with your privacy, but
that's just one of those things, isn't it?'

To her surprise his lips curved in a thin, unfathomable
kind of smile.

'I can assure you, Miss Chapman,' he said evenly, 'that

nothing you can do here, on Surcoufe, will interfere with my privacy.'

So confident his tone! And a challenge in his steady, penetrating gaze. Reyna could not help recalling that odd twinge of uneasiness she had experienced on another occasion; she was affected in the same way now—in fact, what she felt at the moment was more like a premonition that all was not as it appeared. Thor Granville was too confident by far. His manner was that of a person who held all the aces ... and who could play them at any time he liked. Yet surely it must be an act! It couldn't be anything else, decided Reyna, shaking off her anxieties determinedly. She recalled how he had tried to domineer poor old Patch, and suspected he was trying to domineer her, now that she was the owner of the other half of the island.

Well, formidable he might be, with his superior ways and sarcastic tongue, but he could never force her to part with her property. Even had she not felt herself to be bound by her obligation to Patch, she would not be interested in selling, neither to Thor Granville nor to anyone else. She had found the Creole house and she meant to renovate it, furnish it, and use it as a holiday retreat. And if she could let it sometimes to others who wanted to get right away from civilisation for a few weeks a year, then she would be only too happy to do so.

She sent him a sidelong glance; his attention was fixed on a patch of loose coral boulders at his feet and he was so absorbed in the activities of a pretty green gecko which was darting about on its suction pads, looking for insects, that he appeared to have forgotten that she was there at all. Reyna watched his eyes move; her own, following their direction, found that his attention was now with four little ghost crabs which had ventured from their burrows and were moving about on the powdery white sand with incredible speed. Just a little farther on a trailing Morning Glory plant occupied a large area at the back of the shore, its roots' function being to fix the sand, preventing it from being washed away.

Not that there was any movement of the sea here close to the shore at this time; the lagoon in the failing light was a mirror of stainless aquamarine, and the only movement was that of the surf breaking over the reef edge. Shah was still enjoying his particular type of sport even though it was unproductive. The sun was dropping in a blaze of orange and red and russet-gold, painting the casuarinas and takamakas with a film of warmth which was a mixture of colours indescribable in its beauty.

Reyna suddenly felt restless, poised on a plane of isolation. She thought; I wonder where else on earth are a man and a woman alone on a tropical coral island ... And they were enemies, she thought, glancing up again. Perhaps it was as well that they were! Taken aback by her musings, she paused to examine his features in more detail than previously. She noted the aristocratic lines of his face, as arresting as they were inscrutable. She found herself reluctantly admitting that there was a certain attraction in the very remoteness of the man, the unapproachable air which to some women would be a challenge. To succeed in piercing that armour, to scale the wall of his indifference—what a victory that would be!

Was he human beneath that veneer of cold hauteur? Could those strange eyes soften with compassion? Did his heart really beat within its casing of stone? He was certainly unusual, unique, she decided, in the way he could keep himself so totally unemotional and aloof. She felt sure that any other man, finding himself alone with a woman on a romantic island like this, would have been quite unable to remain unaffected by the presence of that woman. Still, it was as well for her that he was cold and unemotional, because there was no denying that she saw something inordinately attractive about him ... She gasped inwardly at her musings and turned away from him as he brought his gaze to her face.

'I must be going,' she said, feeling awkward and tensed in some inexplicable way. The falling shadows seemed to be having a profound yet indefinable effect on her; they were magic, primitive ... enticing ...

There was a strange pause before Thor Granville spoke. It was evident to Reyna as soon as she heard the invitation that he had considered well before extending it.

'I'd like you to join me in a meal, Miss Chapman.'

She looked at him consideringly, wondering why his words had not come as a complete shock to her—and then she understood. He wanted to talk, and make another attempt at persuading her to sell out to him. She hesitated, then shook her head. Much as the idea of a meal tempted, she was not in the mood for an argument. And it would be an argument, since she would be adopting a negative attitude towards his attempts to coerce her into parting with her half of the island.

'Thank you, Mr Granville, but I have to decline your invitation.'

His eyes flickered as he regarded her thoughtfully.

'Will you give me a reason for your refusal to dine with me?' he asked.

'There isn't any need for a reason, Mr Granville. I'm not intending to dine with you, that's all.'

'You obviously know that I want to talk to you,' he said.

'Yes; and as I've already told you, there isn't anything for you and me to talk about.'

She expected him to show anger, or at least impatience. Instead, he changed the subject abruptly, saying, as his glance flickered over her soiled attire,

'You're managing to find something to pass away your time, apparently?'

'I wander around,' she answered casually.

A small silence and then,

'You've found out which is your land by now?'

'Yes,' she replied, 'I have—to some extent, that is.'

'And you realise the impossibility of development taking place without co-operation from me?'

She had to agree, but because he was looking so very satisfied with himself she added that she could still do something regarding tourism.

'I might make it possible for small numbers of people to come for their holidays,' she said. She was only thinking about her villa, but she hoped she had given him the impression that she contemplated building rows of holiday cottages along one of the beautiful palm-fringed beaches.

'And how do you propose to do that, Miss Chapman?' he inquired, lifting a casual hand to stifle a yawn.

Reyna knew a tug of anger at this action, being fully aware that it had been done for effect.

'I'm not prepared to divulge my plans at this time,' she answered, and had the satisfaction of seeing his mouth tighten. He was furious; she could sense it, but as always he retained that air of cool hauteur.

'You're being very obstinate, Miss Chapman. Typically obstinate.'

'What,' she asked, frowning, 'do you mean by typically?'

'Women are notoriously obstinate. It's a pity we have this deplorable equality of the sexes. When a man was within his rights to chastise his womenfolk—be they his wife or his daughters—life ran on much smoother lines for everyone.'

She gasped audibly.

'You're certainly filled with the idea that the male of our species is all and the female nothing!' she flashed. 'It's perhaps as well that you've cut yourself off from the rest of humanity—as Patch said!'

'Patch being your very good friend Mr Harper.' He shook his head in a gesture of impatience. 'Can I ask how you came to inherit his property, Miss Chapman? When

he was here he admitted that he hadn't one close friend—
not one.'

'I became friendly with him, but how and when is no
concern of yours,' she said shortly.

He stood looking down at her in silence for a long
moment before saying,

'Just what do you do with your time here, Miss Chapman?'

The abruptness of the question took her aback, as no
doubt he meant it to. Was he trying to get her off guard so
that she would give him a clue as to why she was in her
present grubby state? If so, he was in for a disappointment!

'That's my business,' she shot back at him without any
attempt at civility.

The grey flecks in his eyes were metallic. She thought:
lord, if I were his wife I'd tremble all over at encountering
an expression like this in his eyes!

'You appear to be intent on making yourself objectionable, Miss Chapman. I assure you that I would make a re-
doubtable opponent if it came to open hostility, so I advise
you to have a care. Your insolent manner is both inexcus-
able and tempting,' he added, and now she saw a thread of
sardonic amusement touch the thin outline of his mouth.
'You appear to forget, Miss Chapman, that you are at my
mercy while you're here, alone with me and with no possible means of getting help no matter how loudly you cried
out for it.'

Her breath caught. She saw the sardonic curve of his
mouth deepen and wondered if she was revealing in some
way the apprehension which his veiled threat had driven
into her. However, she contrived to appear undaunted as,
making no reference to it whatsoever, she said,

'I should have thought we've already reached the point
of open hostility.'

The metal returned to his eyes, those steely glints being

more pronounced than Reyna had yet seen them.

'You'll go too far one of these days!' he snapped and, swinging away, he whistled to Shah to come to heel. The next moment saw him striding along the shore, an angular, formidable figure with arrogant self-possession even in the way he carried himself.

Reyna set her teeth, determined to try and ignore his subtle threats but wishing that he would not be so cryptic. If there was something of which she was in ignorance then why didn't he come right out with it instead of uttering these veiled threats and making remarks whose meanings were obscure?

She made her way to her cabin, her eyes wandering to the lagoon, drowsy as dusk now as the shadows lengthened. What peace! Not a sound other than the breaking of the surf over the edge of the fringing reef and the shrill monotonous song of the cicadas in the casuarina trees behind the shore. A night-flying hawk-moth passed close to her face and then a little blue butterfly hovered near, its wings iridescent even in the reduced light of approaching dusk.

What would it be like to live here? She felt she could have renounced everything and settled here if only there were not so many snags. Thor Granville for one thing, of course; impossible to have him as a neighbour. Then there was the all-important matter of money. She smiled as she entered the cabin. Dreams were only dreams, but they were enjoyable while they lasted—dreams like the one she had just been indulging in.

Reality faced her immediately she entered. Fruit was very nice . . . as an extra! Water was wonderful . . . when you were really thirsty. A sigh escaped her as she took from her rucksack the bananas and the pineapple she had brought in for her evening meal. But when she went to the water jug she was dismayed to find that a wasp had dropped into the water and was floating on the surface.

'Now what do I do?' She could never drink water that

had been contaminated like that, even though it might well be safe to do so. She was still thirsty after eating her fruit and after another small hesitation she decided to go to the lovely white villa and ask Thor Granville for another jugful of water. He would probably snub her, but she was past caring. The water was more important than her pride at this moment.

CHAPTER FIVE

THE delicious smell of steak cooking assailed Reyna's nostrils long before she reached the back door of Thor Granville's house. And by the time she did reach her destination her mouth was watering. The door was wide open, the room brightly lit from a centre light in the ceiling and a light running the full length of a long unit, the top of which was white formica and the cupboards and drawers beneath were of highly polished albizia wood which was white in colour. Reyna stood a moment before tapping on the door, her appreciative feminine gaze finding everything anyone could want in the way of modern conveniences. She had seen the kitchen before, of course, but had never stopped to stare in case Thor Granville had come from another room and seen her. Now, however, she allowed herself a moment or two to take it all in. Pale blue walls and pretty striped curtains in blue and white; a white breakfast set consisting of a round table on which was spread a blue and white cloth, and four chairs of albizia wood with pale blue upholstered seats. On a shelf were about half a dozen bottles of wine, and another bottle cooling in an ice bucket.

He certainly did himself well! Reyna felt that there was a good deal that she did not understand about this whole situation. This man was an enigma to her, being very different from what she had imagined from Patch's description of him. She had expected Thor Granville to be somewhat uncouth, not too particular as to personal cleanliness. She had taken it for granted that a man as avaricious as he would be bound to have his greed written into the lines of his face. Instead, she had met a man of cultured taste, of aristocratic feature and bearing, and he was also fastidious

78

as regards cleanliness, she decided, her glance moving swiftly around the kitchen again. And suddenly she was intrigued; she wanted to learn something about him—his background, his life before coming to Surcoufe, and the reason why he was here now. She was beginning to find flaws in Patch's story, but she was unable to see clearly where the flaws lay.

So carried away was she by her thoughts that she actually jumped when Thor Granville, coming into the kitchen, said, in terse and formal accents,

'What can I do for you, Miss Chapman?'

His eyes went quite automatically to the jug she held in her hand, and even before she spoke he was preparing to take it from her.

'If I could have some water——' she murmured self-consciously. How immaculate he looked—in a white linen suit and with his hair gleaming, newly-washed, she felt sure. Looking down deprecatingly at her own attire, Reyna felt inadequate, inferior. 'I left the cover off the jug and an insect got into it.' Did he believe her? she wondered. He was looking a little sceptical, she thought. The smell of the steak—which she realised was under the grill—was a subtle form of torture because it had the effect of making her aware of just how hungry she was. She could smell vegetables, too—cauliflower and carrots, she thought, and something that could be onion sauce . . .

'Certainly.' He took the jug, then changed his mind and handed it back to her. 'Help yourself,' he said. 'You usually do.'

She stepped inside, feeling more awkward than ever.

'Do you get your water from a well?' she asked, in an endeavour to hide her loss of confidence.

'Yes; it's pumped up electrically.'

'An electric pump. It seems impossible that you have all these things here, on an island so far from anywhere.' She was at the sink, subconsciously noticing its highly-polished surface. It was stainless steel and looked almost new. She glanced at the grill, which was over the gleaming cooker, and swallowed the saliva that had gathered as a result of the tantalising odours pervading the air around her.

'Have you had your meal?' inquired Thor Granville unexpectedly.

She nodded quickly.

'Yes, I have.'

He glanced at the jug, which was now full of water.

'And now it's coffee time. I suppose?'

She sent him a kindling glance.

'Water never did anyone any harm!' she snapped.

'Miss Chapman,' he said ignoring this, 'if you care to change your mind about that invitation, you are welcome to join me for dinner.' Smooth, suave, and certainly condescending his voice and manner, and in addition there was the merest hint of satire in those lazy topaz eyes of his. Reyna bit her lip, stifling the swift refusal that was born of pride. Yet she hesitated, hunger battling with the reluctance to lose face. But hunger always wins, she told herself as an excuse when presently she found herself saying,

'Thank you, Mr Granville, I will have dinner with you.'

Unexpectedly he held out a hand and took the jug from her.

'You might want to wash and brush up? You'll find the bathroom along the passage. Turn right out of here.'

'Thank you,' she answered dazedly. What an unpredictable man he was! Oh, yes, he was condescending, and he was secretly laughing at her, and what was more, he was scheming to begin that act of coercion again. But there was nothing actually malicious about him—at least, not at this moment. In admitting this Reyna became more curious about him. This house was so spotlessly clean, but Thor Granville was certainly not the kind of man to do his own housework! Too superior by far, with that air of distinction and hauteur. But if he didn't do his own housework then who did? Smiling to herself as she made her way to the bathroom, she did wonder why she should be wasting so much thought on the man. What she ought to be concentrating on was that juicy steak she would be eating shortly.

She found the bathroom as well planned as the rest of the house, and as luxurious—with its avocado green suite and matching curtains and carpet, its gold-plated fittings and primrose walls. It had a distinctly masculine flavour about it, with the trace of after-shave lotion in the air which reminded Reyna of the tang of a mountain breeze or the mysterious, elusive perfume that comes drifting over heather moors in autumn.

She looked longingly at the bath, then ran warm water into the basin and washed her hands and face. Her comb happened to be in the pocket of her jeans, so she was able to tidy her hair. She wished she had something else to wear and vaguely wondered why her appearance should trouble her. After all, there was no one to look at her. Certainly Thor Granville wouldn't be interested in her appearance. Nor did she want him to be. Far safer to be ignored!

He was at the stove when she returned to the kitchen, sticking a fork into the steak which he had just taken from under the heat.

'How do you like yours?' he asked casually over his shoulder.

'Well cooked, please.'

'Then you'd better come and do it yourself. I tend to under-cook for other people, especially when they like their steak well done.'

'So you entertain?' The question was out before Reyna could stop it and he swung around, his expression faintly amused. Lord! The man was just too attractive altogether when he dropped his austerity like this!

'I'm not quite the hermit which your friend Harper described to you, Miss Chapman. However, let's get back to this steak. I've brought a piece from the deep-freeze, but it's not thawed out, obviously. Put it under the grill, and then perhaps you'd like a drink while we're waiting?'

Automatically she moved to the stove. The steak was on a plate, so she put it under the grill, aware that he was busy stirring the sauce. It was strange to see so masculine a man standing at a stove. But if he chose a life like this then he must of necessity do his own cooking. She glanced at his long flexible fingers and decided he had an artistic streak in him. Without doubt he was a man of varied and distinctive attributes.

A few minutes later she was in the sitting-room where a table had been laid by the smaller of two windows.

'I don't trouble to use the dining-room when I'm on my own,' he explained. 'My music's in here and I like to listen while I eat.'

The wine was on the table, which was laid with thick, heavily-embroidered mats, gleaming silver and fine china. He had already laid her place and was now at the cupboard, ready to pour her her drink.

'What would you like, Miss Chapman?'

'Dry sherry, please,' she answered, wishing she was not feeling under such an obligation to him.

Half an hour later they were seated at the table and Reyna, ravenously hungry as she was, had some considerable difficulty in exercising her customary good manners. But she contrived to eat slowly, and she savoured every mouthful, aware that she would be on her diet of fruit tomorrow.

'More wine?' Thor as a host was fastidious in his concern, making sure she had everything she required. She was seeing an attractive side of him which brought on the thought that he must surely have had some experience of women. At thirty-five it seemed impossible that he had not had at least one serious love-affair. He appeared far too attractive to have been able to escape women altogether. He was holding the bottle, waiting for her answer, and she nodded, saying yes, she would like some more wine.

She lifted the glass; it caught a reflection from a standard lamp and sent sparks of light shooting against the silver cruet in the centre of the table. She thought: it needs only flowers and candles for this to be the most romantic setting in which a meal could ever be eaten. She sipped her drink, lost in thought, and then, conscious of his critical stare, she took a proper drink of her wine.

'Is the steak to your liking?' he asked, breaking the silence which had settled between them. 'You didn't overcook it?' He eyed it with a slight frown; she had noticed that his steak was very rare.

'It's delicious,' she answered and, to herself, she was saying that it was the most delicious meal she had eaten for years! But never would she have given him the satisfaction of knowing just how much she was appreciating his hospitality.

'Good. Help yourself to more vegetables if you want them.'

'Thank you, I will.'

The main course was followed by a trifle—a scrumptious-looking affair topped with walnuts and whipped cream.

'From the deep-freeze,' offered Thor Granville in some amusement as he noticed Reyna's expression as he put it on the table and told her to help herself. 'Frozen foods are the biggest boon of the century.'

She looked at him in surprise, wondering what had brought about this dramatic change in his attitude towards her. It encouraged her to say that she agreed about the frozen foods, and could not resist adding,

'They've made the lot of the housewife so much easier, haven't they?'

'I expect so,' without much interest. 'I was speaking about myself. I find that as long as I see that the deep-freeze is kept stocked, I'm not short of anything I could have if I lived on Mahé.'

'Perhaps, one day, I shall be able to make my own electricity,' she mused, speaking her thoughts aloud. 'And then I can have these modern conveniences which you have.' In her dreams she saw the Creole villa, growing a little through the years as she added a modern kitchen and a small extra building for such things as the deep-freeze she had mentioned and other domestic aids. The excitement bred by anticipation brought a glow to her eyes and a smile to her lips. Thor Granville's expression was suddenly a frowning one and his voice was taut when presently he said,

'You'd live here?'

'I'd love to, but it isn't poss——' She broke off, biting her lip in vexation. She had made a slip that could give the perceptive Thor Granville a clue to her finances. His eyes were narrowed, she noticed, and his manner was one of faint contempt. He said quietly,

'Help yourself to trifle, Miss Chapman. It has to be finished up.' He watched her take a second helping before he spoke again. 'And why, might I ask, is it not possible for you to live here?'

She had her answer ready; it had come to her in a flash.

'It wouldn't be the thing, would it, just you and me on an otherwise uninhabited island?'

The topaz eyes flickered strangely.

'But you've been telling me, Miss Chapman, that it's your intention to have tourists here,' he reminded her gently.

She coloured, floundering about for a suitable response to this, but of course she found none.

'I suppose,' she said at last with a hint of defiance, 'that I was thinking of now—when there are no tourists.'

'But now, when there are no tourists, you haven't a house, so how are you to have these modern conveniences you mention? You can scarcely have them in your present dwelling,' he added in some amusement.

She averted her head, her eyes on the trifle on her plate. It was quite incredible, but she found herself on the verge of making a full confession, admitting that she had no money and that, even if she had, nothing would induce her to ravage even one square yard of this lovely island. Instead, she merely said,

'Perhaps it was a stupid thing for me to say, Mr Granville. I was carried away by all I've seen here, in your beautiful house.'

There was a moment of silence and then,

'If you've finished we'll sit over there, on the verandah, and have our coffee.' The far window, fixed in a long sliding stainless steel frame, was wide open and the verandah was on the other side of it, facing the gardens, the beach and then the lagoon and beyond this the dark unfathomable expanse of sea. Lights on the verandah revealed exotic flowers in urns and ornamental earthenware pots, and at one end a bougainvillaea tumbled its blossoms over a rustic trellis, behind which was another light providing a very subtle glow.

As soon as they were settled down with the pot of steaming coffee on the table, Thor Granville spoke, and now his voice changed dramatically, becoming brisk and business-like and, in consequence, a trifle curt.

'Miss Chapman, I feel this is a suitable opportunity for us to discuss the fate of this island. I want to buy your half and I'm willing to give you what, in my opinion, is a fair price—the price in fact which I offered to your friend. He was an obstinate old man with ideas of his own regarding my villainy, but this is all in the past and of no value anyway in this discussion.' He paused a moment to push the silver sugar box towards her, and then he passed her the matching cream jug. 'I was hoping to have purchased the property by correspondence, taking it for granted that you wouldn't want to hold on to it, as it was of no practical value to you—as I mentioned in my letter.'

Reyna remembered that assumptive communication vividly; she also remembered its effect on her temper. She had been so furious that even if she had contemplated selling her half of the island, she would never have dreamed of offering it to him. The letter had been altogether too hostile in its content, too unfriendly, and in addition the impression it gave was that the writer was a domineering, aggressive sort of man who fitted to perfection the picture of Thor Granville she had put together from the description given her by Patch.

And now, as he mentioned it again, she felt a surge of anger rise within her and it was with difficulty that she hid her feelings as she said quietly,

'I have no intention of selling my half of Surcoufe, Mr Granville. I've already told you this several times, and nothing can make me change my mind. No offer you can put forward would interest me in the least.' She felt a tinge of regret that this subject had come up, for the evening so far had been pleasant in the extreme. She had enjoyed an excellent meal and now she was enjoying the cool breeze while sitting here, in this heavenly place, drinking delicious coffee and trying not to think of her cabin with its truckle bed, or the breakfast of bananas and pineapples she would be having in the morning.

She saw her companion's mouth tighten, and noticed the steely glints become more pronounced as his eyes settled on her face. She thought of his name and wondered, not for the first time, if he had Norwegian blood in his veins. Thor, she recalled, was the Norse god of thunder, but he had also prevailed over every other god, so became in the end the most important of the pagan deities. As Reyna continued to stare at Thor Granville now she found her imagination running away with her, for in the shadows cast by the leafy tangle of a bougainvillaea vine as the glow from the lamp filtered through it in irregular splotches, she had no difficulty at all in describing his austere profile as pagan in appearance. She thought of poor old Patch, trying in vain to combat this man's dominating personality, and being driven, in the end, from his own property.

'Miss Chapman,' he said after a long pause during which he seemed to be debating some problem of his own, 'I am determined to own this island. I strongly advise you to give in gracefully and sell out to me.'

She frowned, her mind bewildered and uneasy because of his confidence, of the firm statement that he was determined to own the island. She felt startled by the fact that anger had not risen again, but there seemed no room for anger as so many other emotions occupied her. For one thing, she was discovering—not without some reluctance—that her antagonism against this man was decreasing all the time. True, he had treated her somewhat badly in that he had made her sleep in that tiny log cabin, and feed on what the island could provide, but apart from that he had not been nearly as objectionable as she had been led by Patch to expect. Although he wanted her half of the island he had not tried to bully her in any way.

'I won't sell, Mr Granville,' she said at last. 'You mystify me by your confidence, and I would ask you to tell me if there's anything about this inheritance that I don't understand.'

He drew an impatient breath, and sat considering for a long moment, his eyes vacant—or so it seemed to Reyna as she sat there watching him staring out to sea. She followed the direction of his gaze, saw a light flickering on the horizon and wondered what kind of a ship it was out there, in the absolute loneliness and darkness of the night.

'Tell me,' said Thor Granville, returning his attention to her, 'is half an island, situated here so great a distance from your home, of any use to you at all?'

'I shall use it as I've said, to—to . . .' She tailed off, quite unable to continue with the deception she had begun when she first encountered this man.

'Yes?' he prompted curtly.

'Nothing,' she sighed. 'I am not selling. Can we please leave it at that?'

'No, we can't, Miss Chapman! I want the whole of this island!'

'You won't get it, Mr Granville.'

She glanced away, avoiding the anger that marked his features. It was a surpassingly beautiful night, and it seemed all wrong to be in a state of contention like this. You didn't fight people when you lived in paradise!

'You'll sell out to me in the end, Miss Chapman,' her companion was saying, his quiet voice tinged with anger and impatience. 'You asked me just now if there was anything you didn't understand. There's much you don't understand, but for the present I'm not willing to enlighten you—— No, don't interrupt!' he told her sternly as she opened her mouth to speak. 'We'll leave the matter in abeyance for the time being. Enjoy your coffee. We'll bring the subject up another time.' Abrupt now, his tone, and final. He had adopted a masterful, arbitrary attitude which forbade any argument. Reyna coloured slightly and picked up her coffee cup. In addition to the coffee and liqueurs which Thor Granville had put on the table there was a small silver-gilt bowl containing a variety of mouth-watering sweetmeats. Reyna had not touched them, although she wanted to. Thor Granville lifted the dish, holding it out to her.

'Thank you very much——' She broke off with sudden shyness, aware of those unusual eyes fixed upon her face.

She popped the confection into her mouth, wondering why she felt so tensed. Her pulses were unsteady, her nerves taut. She found herself grappling with a sensation she had never before experienced. Her mind was confused but at the same time stimulated in some indefinable way. The wine had been heady, she recalled, deciding she ought not to have had it, seeing that for the past three days there had been no real solid food in her diet.

Thor Granville broke the silence at length, casually saying,

'Tell me a little about yourself, Miss Chapman. Do you live at home with your parents, or are you one of those independent young women who've broken away from home to make your own way in life?'

'I have no parents,' she replied, a little taken aback at his interest but at the same time glad that he had said something to take her mind off those strange and rather troublesome sensations. She hated to be baffled by anything ... especially by her own feelings. 'An aunt brought me up.' She went on to tell him about her Aunt Saran and how she came to have that particular name. He nodded as if impatient of irrelevancies and Reyna sank once more into silence.

'Your parents left you a fortune, I take it?' Thor Granville's voice cut into the silence again, startling her with the unexpected question.

'No—er—yes, they d-did,' she stammered, colouring painfully as, noticing the censorious lift of an eyebrow, she was left in no doubt at all that he knew she was lying.

'I thought they must have done,' he returned casually. 'Because otherwise you wouldn't have been contemplating development here.'

Sarcasm again, but malicious this time. He intended to make her feel small—and he had succeeded. She changed the subject abruptly, saying that she ought to be thinking of leaving and making her way back to her cabin.

'It's early yet. What do you do in there for twelve hours or so?'

'I lie down and—well—think,' she answered with a wan little smile.

'Think about what?'

'This place, mostly,' she answered truthfully. 'I think it's very beautiful. Just look at that scene there——' She pointed to the sea where it rode the edge of the coral reef. 'The wonders of nature . . .' She trailed off, aware that she had been carried away.

'Tell me some more about your impressions,' he invited.

'About the reef, you mean, and the lagoon?' He merely nodded and she went on, vaguely stunned by the knowledge that she wanted to prolong her stay here, with this man . . . 'Have you ever thought how many millions of tiny creatures have gone to the making of that reef? And don't you see that it's one of the wonders of nature that the living coral adapts itself to whatever environment it happens to be in? Take the far side of the reef, for instance, where the waves break more violently over it: there you'll find the tougher species like the stinging coral; then on the reef edge you have more delicate corals like the stag's horn and the pretty sea fans. On the landward side of the reef where it's well protected from the breaking of the surf, you can find the brain coral and the favids . . .' Reyna let her voice trail away to silence as she noticed the strange expression in Thor Granville's eyes.

'Most interesting,' he commented in a rather dry voice. 'You've obviously at some time or other studied the formation of coral reefs?' It was a statement rather than a question, but he was plainly expecting an answer.

'Er—yes, I have,' she admitted hesitantly. It had never occurred to her that in talking about her favourite subject —geology—she might just be giving him a hint regarding her occupation.

'And one doesn't study coral reefs without other aspects of nature, does one?' he said gently.

'I don't know what you mean, Mr Granville.'

'I rather think you do, Miss Chapman.' He leant forward to pick up the bon-bon dish. 'Have another. I never eat them myself, so you may as well finish them; they're never the same once they've been taken out of their box.'

She sent him a speaking glance.

'Thank you,' she snapped, and then, because she could not help it, 'Do you always adopt this cryptic way with your acquaintances, Mr Granville?'

To her surprise he laughed.

'The game we play is amusing. I wonder which of us will show our hand first?' The lazy topaz eyes glimmered with humour and, looking into them, Reyna felt an inexplicable quickening of the blood in her veins and for a moment she was too bewildered to speculate on what he had just said. But she did say eventually, her thoughts shooting off at a tangent as she tried to cope with several sensations at once,

'Game, Mr Granville? Are you being cryptic again?'

'No, Miss Chapman,' came the swift counter-attack, 'it's you who are being obtuse ... or shall we say you're pretending to be obtuse?' The voice was gently sarcastic, the thin lips curled in a smile that was almost a sneer. 'Can I give you some more coffee?'

Reyna swallowed hard. It was too disconcerting by far, this man's subtleness in the way he was treating her. She said, but with some difficulty,

'Yes, please, I would like some more.'

'And another liqueur?'

This time she shook her head.

'No, thank you.' She watched him pour the coffee, noticing again the slender flexible fingers with their immaculately-tended nails. She turned away, deeply affected by her emotions, emotions which she tried to understand but failed. She looked out over the shadowed gardens and wondered if it was the magical unreality of her situation that caused this tumult within her. All was so silent out there where everything drowsed in this long-drawn-out tropical night with the moon hanging low in an inky sky and a zephyr of a breeze drifting in from the Indian Ocean to stir the palm fronds. In the hauntingly beautiful sky over the lagoon a million stars shone, blinking at the moon, while far away in the unfathomable distance the arc of the heavens was a mystic realm of crowded constellations.

So far from the world of reality! Two people alone on an island, a primitive, languorous island floating like a jewel on the soft dark waters of the lagoon. On the shore the waves lapped silently, caressingly ... Moths fluttered in the sweet-scented air around the verandah, and on the wall two dainty green lizards darted about, chasing insects.

A man and a woman on an island ...

She glanced at the man sitting there, opposite to her, his features as dark and unmoving as the shadow in which they were caught. Reyna was conscious of an intangible longing within her and knew it had something to do with Thor Granville. She attempted to ignore it, and reached for her coffee cup. His eyes moved, to become riveted on her face. The moment became fraught with tension as some unfathomable vibration seemed to pass right through her, tightening her nerves. She noticed his eyes widen a little and caught her breath, wondering if the intensity of her impressions was in some way revealed to him. She took a drink, then, replacing the cup on its saucer, she said it was time she was going.

'I'll walk with you,' he offered casually. 'It's very dark along my path, and even darker in the cedar forest.'

'Thank you.' She was not sure whether she wanted him to walk her through the cedar forest, even though the thought of going through it alone had been causing her a tinge of apprehension each time she thought about it. 'I saw a snake yesterday, in the little clearing near my cabin.'

'Don't worry about them. We have no poisonous snakes in the Seychelles.'

He had risen, and Reyna followed him back into the house. She watched him close the long window, heard him say he would fetch a torch, and all the time she was wrestling with the confusion of her mind, endeavouring to analyse her feelings. He returned carrying a long powerful torch; a few minutes later they had left the grounds of the villa and were walking through the cedar forest. Thor Granville directed the long beam of his torch on the path as absolute darkness enclosed them. But when the canopy of foliage thinned the moonlight sufficed and he turned off the torchlight. Reyna, caught in a spell from which she had no desire to escape, knew a little thrill of pleasure when, accidentally, her companion's hand, swinging at his side, touched hers. She glanced upwards, casting him a covert glance. His profile was firm and noble, etched darkly against the argent shafts of moonlight filtering through the trees.

'Here we are.' Thor Granville switched on his torch again as he opened the cabin door for her. 'You can take this——' He held out the torch, which she accepted without any demur, saying gratefully,

'Thank you, Mr Granville. I do appreciate the loan of it.'

He seemed to frown, but she was not sure. All he said was,

'Good night, Miss Chapman, sleep well.'

'Good night, Mr Granville. And thank you very much for a lovely meal.'

'Don't mention it.' The finely-timbred voice took on a sardonic edge as he continued, 'You obviously guessed, when I first asked you to dine with me, that it was a calculated approach on my part in order to create a suitable atmosphere for a discussion on the fate of your half of this island. I hoped to persuade you to sell. However, although we didn't manage to come to an agreement, we did manage a pause in our aggressiveness towards one another, with the result that the evening passed very pleasantly indeed. I think you will agree about that, Miss Chapman?'

'Yes—er—yes,' she stammered, her heart leaping wildly

at this frank admission on the part of the austere Thor Granville. Her eyes glowed in the moonlight, meeting his shyly, hesitantly, and her lips parted in a smile that lingered, bringing the most odd expression to her companion's eyes. Was it perception? she wondered. Perception of what? His brow creased slowly and he was frowning, his lips pursed; and it did seem that an inner, silent exclamation of annoyance was uttered.

'It—it is nice of you to say s-so,' she murmured, feeling small and inadequate and gauche. 'Er—good night,' she said again. What was the matter with her? Surely she was not going to have a crush on the man!

A crush . . . She stood by the open door of the cabin and watched him stride away, a tall assured figure with the spring of an athlete in his step. He was soon lost to sight and she turned, quite unconsciously putting a hand to her heart. A crush? No, she admitted, dazed by the revelation that had come to her, it was something far more disturbing than that . . .

CHAPTER SIX

THE long beam of the torch penetrated the interior of the cabin as Reyna entered. She was still dazed, her mind in a ferment because although she was unable to accept that she was emotionally affected by Thor Granville, she was honest enough not to make any emphatic denial.

A sudden movement caught her eye and she gasped, standing stock still, her pupils dilating at the sight of the giant centipede—more than eight inches long, she estimated—that was moving with sinuous lack of effort towards the place where her pillow was covered with the blanket. Instinct caused her to run from the cabin, but once outside she knew she would have to enter it again and, gritting her teeth, she went back. The creature had disappeared; she had visions of its being in the bed and a shudder rippled through her. Nevertheless, she was able to snatch the blanket and pull it from the bed. No sign of the centipede.

She knew that sleep would be denied her—even if she had the courage to get into bed knowing the creature was still in the cabin. In the hope that it might—like moths and flies—follow a light, she stepped out once more and stood there, the torchlight trained on the ground just outside the doorway. She had been waiting optimistically for some moments when she heard the rustling of footsteps on the vegetation behind her. Thor Granville said quietly,

'Is something wrong? I saw your light outside the cabin as I turned out of the wood.'

Reyna swung round, unintentionally directing the beam on to his face. She had a fleeting glimpse of stern taut features, and the slight furrow on his brow indicative of a frown of puzzlement.

'It's a centipede,' she explained a trifle selfconsciously. 'It's huge——' She broke off, aware that he could be secretly laughing at her feminine timidity. 'Perhaps it's quite harmless——'

'They can give you a nasty bite. Where is it?'

'It was on the bed.' She gestured vaguely. 'It's gone; I can't find it.'

'You should have killed it right away. They're vicious little brutes. I had an eye closed for over a week after being bitten by one of them.' Taking the torch from her, Thor stepped into the cabin. Reyna stood in the doorway, her gaze on his broad back as he bent to make a thorough examination of the bed. After a while he straightened up, and she thought she heard a little sign of resignation escape from his lips. However, he stopped again, the light from the torch travelling slowly along the wall where it met the floor. At last he turned and looked at her. 'It's obviously somewhere about; but I can't find it.' Again there seemed to be a sigh of resignation. 'You'd better sleep in one of my spare bedrooms.'

Silence. Something tight and tense gripped at Reyna's nerve-ends, causing her to hesitate before accepting his offer. Alongside her hesitation was the conviction that she could never sleep in the cabin while the centipede was there.

'What's the matter?' Sardonic amusement tinged Thor Granville's voice and Reyna knew she flushed slightly in the darkness. It was plain that he had guessed the reason for her hesitation.

'Nothing.' She hoped her voice sounded casual. 'It's good of you to offer me the room.'

He came from the cabin, pulling the door to behind him.

'The only logical thing to do,' he responded carelessly. 'I don't want you ill on my hands.'

'Would I really be ill?' she asked, glancing up into his face.

'As I said, this type of centipede is vicious. They bite you for no reason at all. Yes, you could be ill.' He was already moving away from the cabin and Reyna fell into step beside him, her feelings very mixed, owing mainly to her sensations of a short while ago when, most reluctantly, she had half-admitted to being attracted to him in the sort of way that could greatly disturb her peace of mind.

'I feel I'm putting you to a lot of trouble,' apologised Reyna after a pause.

'Upsetting my smooth-running bachelor existence?' There appeared to be a tinge of amusement in his voice and again she shot a glance at his profile. It was a silhouette in the moonlight, sharply etched and formidable but with a silght curve to the mouth which could have been the hint of a smile. Reyna made no comment on what he had said and they strolled along in silence for some time. All was so still and hushed—even the cicadas seemed to be slumbering. The lagoon, drowsy and motionless, lay like a sheet of glass painted with silver. The palms fluttered reluctantly, as if resenting the breeze that disturbed their peace. Magic was there in abundance. Tropical trees lining the shore of a coral island which lay in serene isolation on the mystic waters of the Indian Ocean. A lagoon and a reef, a millon stars in a sky of deep purple, an enormous moon to light the way through a sleepy cedar forest. All this ... and a man and a woman walking side by side ...

So far away that medieval inn where it had all begun! So unreal such things as England, and the school, and children like Jimmy Lloyd.

Reyna, caught in the magic, knew a restlessness that strove for understanding. This was too much; she ought to be here with a lover. The setting was wasted ...

It was with a deep sigh of relief that she saw the lights of the villa appear through the trees. Here was reality; a structure made by man. Only Nature was magic; man was prosaic, logical, coldly realistic.

The villa was as bright as when she had left it, with the verandah lights still on as well as those inside. Reyna entered the kitchen and turned, watching Thor Granville close the door. There was no need for a lock or a bolt, and the door was merely on the latch.

'Come,' invited Thor, placing the torch on the table. 'I'm not sure whether the bed's made up or not.'

'I—can do it.' She was shy, hesitant as she followed him along a corridor. His manner was pleasant, with not a trace of the impatience which, under these circumstances, would have been more understandable.

The room was most attractive in the rose-coloured glow from the bed lamp which Thor snapped on after entering. He flicked down the bed cover and nodded with satisfaction.

'Yes, it's all ready for getting into.' He looked down at her, standing rather diffidently in the doorway. 'You know where the bathroom is. The water's hot if you want to take a bath. I'll get you some towels.'

'But you—er—won't you want the bath?' She had never felt so shy and awkward in the whole of her life. 'I mean, it'll inconvenience you if I have a bath.'

'I shan't need it yet awhile. I never go to bed before midnight.'

'Oh, well—thank you. I certainly would enjoy a bath.'

'In that case,' he said in some amusement, 'I'd better let you have a dressing-gown.'

Reyna opened her mouth to protest, then closed it again, realising that there was no sense in refusing his offer.

He went away and she entered the bedroom, noticing the expensive curtains, the highly-polished tiled floor upon which lay several white lambskin rugs. The walls were white, the furniture of the pleasant yellow wood of the

jacquier tree. On the bed was a white folkweave spread
with an ornamental fringe intricately knotted where it
joined the spread.

Thor Granville returned with the towels and a bright red
silk dressing-gown over his arm.

'A trifle too large, no doubt, but the best I could do at
such short notice.' The good humour in his voice could not
possibly escape Reyna and her nerves caught. The man was
altogether too attractive in a mood like this . . . dangerously
attractive.

He handed her the dressing-gown along with the towels,
his glance sweeping the room as if he were making sure she
had all she could require. 'Use what you like in the bathroom,' he told her. 'I think you'll find all that's necessary.'

She coloured daintily, averting her eyes. Impossible to be
natural in such unnatural circumstances. Thor seemed to
want to ease this confusion, for he said lightly, 'Good night,
Miss Chapman, and happy dreams!'

She smiled then, murmured another thank you and
stood watching as he made his departure from the room.

Five minutes later she was in the bath, savouring the
luxury of lying there, the warm soapy water covering her
body. It was nice to think that she could stay as long as she
liked, and that when she came out she would have a proper
bed to sleep in.

It was more than half an hour before she emerged from
the steam and warmth of the bathroom, her slender frame
buried in the red silk dressing-gown. Along the passage was
the kitchen and something made her tread silently towards
the light. Thor was putting the dinner plates and other
crockery into a dish-washing machine. He glanced up before she could escape. She opened her mouth to bid him
good night, but his laugh halted the words.

'Very chic,' he declared. 'Red suits you.'

Reyna found herself flushing with pleasure.

'I think so too; I must start wearing it.'

Thor straightened up, immaculate as ever despite the chore he had been performing.

'So much for modern science,' he commented with a glance at the machine.

'Yes, they're all right, aren't they? I haven't one yet, but one day...' She tailed off, biting her lip as she saw the hint of sardonic amusement on his face. She waited for some remark that would embarrass her, but instead, after a small moment of considering, she heard him say,

'Perhaps you'd like a nightcap?'

The invitation startled her; she knew she ought to refuse, but some force stronger than caution impelled her to accept.

'It's kind of you, Mr Granville,' she said, and immediately saw laughter in his eyes.

'Being polite, eh? Well, I suppose you feel you have to be. I'm not kind, though,' he warned, and now his tones were as serious as they could be. 'I can be very unscrupulous, as you'll find if you don't come to my way of thinking.'

'As regards selling out to you?'

His eyes flickered over her face; she thought she saw a hint of admiration there.

'Tell me,' he said unexpectedly changing the subject, 'have you a boy-friend?'

'Sort of,' she replied casually.

'Nothing serious, then?'

She shook her head.

'No, nothing serious.' It was a strange thing, but she could not even bring Kevin's face into focus. He had become a nebulous figure, totally unimportant to her now.

'Come into the living-room,' he invited, gesturing towards the door. 'We'll have our drink in there.'

He left the light on in the kitchen; she followed him into the room in which they had eaten the delicious meal only a couple of hours ago. In response to a flick of his hand she sank down into the big armchair, frowning at her attire, wishing, womanlike, that she were dressed in something more becoming than Thor Granville's dressing-gown.

Suddenly, without warning, the light failed.

'Damn!' came the exclamation through the darkness. 'This is the second time in a week!' He threw back the curtains and the moonlight streamed into the room, highlighting the bottles in the cabinet whose doors were wide open. Reyna glanced at Thor and their eyes held for a long moment that seemed to stretch to the very edge of eternity. The atmosphere in the room was tense; plucked were Reyna's nerves, and her heart was racing in unison with the increased rate of her pulse. In a moment of sheer peril she tried to collect her thoughts, to move away as he came towards her, as if drawn against his will. He paused only to replace the bottle he held, placing it on top of the cabinet. And then he was standing close to her, towering above her. Her face, wreathed in the moon's silver effulgence, looked pale, ethereal; her lips were parted, her thoughts wildly confused. Was it the sheer glory of the moonlight that caused her blood to race so madly through her veins? Or was it this moment of peril, and of temptation?

Thor reached out a hand and Reyna had no power of movement as he took hold of hers, no primitive urge to escape, to avoid what she knew instinctively was to come. Yet when Thor did take her to him his action shook her nerves with the thrill of the unexpected. She was drawn to his arms so that her breasts were crushed against him; she wondered if he could feel the wild palpitation of her heart. Her whole body quivered against him as he bent to kiss her, his lips warm, sensuous, masterfully forcing hers apart. She felt the tip of his tongue against hers and every single nerve in her body tingled with the excitement that only ecstasy can bring. He held her away at last, his warm hands on her arms, his perceptive eyes faintly smiling ... with triumph.

'I—I—please let me g-go.' Could anything have been more half-hearted? she wondered, fully expecting that smile in his eyes to deepen, which it did.

'Go?' with a lift of his straight dark brows—those satanic brows of which Patch had spoken. 'Can you honestly say you mean that?'

She bit her lip, unable to lie. Yet she knew that one half of her wanted to escape—the cautious, logical half. The other craved to be captured, and brought to the exquisite submission of complete surrender. This island was made for love. Never in her life had Reyna been so affected by her surroundings, been in the grip of some force that seemed to be drawing her into the abandonment of physical desire. To encourage him would be easy ... or would it? She had had no experience. Yet the impulse to act like a sheer wanton was so strong that it almost took complete possession of her. She *wanted* him ...

To lead him on by a caress—just the tender touch of her hand on his cheek, or his throat ... to lift her face and offer her lips in supplication ...

Shame fought with desire, self-disgust with the magnetism of the man whose hands were firmly holding her shoulders. His head came down again, and his lips took hers in a kiss even more primitive and demanding than the first. Reyna relaxed her body, gave herself up for lost and cast aside the tiny thread of warning that there was tomorrow to be faced ... tomorrow when she would be unable to come anywhere near to Thor, so steeped in shame would she be.

Suddenly, without warning, Thor released her and said brusquely,

'I'll go and see what's wrong with the generator.'

She watched his figure disappear through the door, every nerve in her body quivering with the sense of anticlimax. Was she glad to escape? The question was by-passed as she realised that her chief emotion was that of anxiety as to what Thor Granville thought of her. He must have guessed that an easy victory would have been achieved had he attempted to take her. And yet ... she was not in love with him, merely attracted physically, that was all.

Filled with shame and embarrassment, Reyna knew an impulse to fly, back to her cabin and the seclusion it afforded, the cabin where, she had already guessed, poor old Patch had stayed while he was on the island.

But instead of escaping—which would have been absurd, anyway, clad as she was in Thor's dressing-gown, she went to the small window and threw it open, feeling the fresh-scented breeze on her hot face; its cool softness was balm to her senses and she stood, her head against the frame, feeling she was alone on the island ... alone and at peace.

Her glance strayed to the shore and the immense dark trees that bordered it—palms and casuarinas and the taka-makas. The breeze freshened as she stood there; it gave her a sense of purity, of total freedom from all that was wrong—or even doubtful. The moon was high, its reflection mirrored on the drowsy lagoon like an enormous jewel, there for the taking; while farther on, the swirling skeins of water made a silver fringe as the surf broke over the reef. Reyna's thoughts were dreamy; she found herself mentally repeating what had registered so profoundly before: a sleepy lagoon and a coral reef, a palm-fringed beach of pure white sand ... a tropical island occupied by a man and a woman. Drifting on the single thread of a forgotten dream came her aunt's warning that two on an island spelt temptation with a capital T. It was all too much—too achingly perilous ... and alluring. The very atmosphere was filled with everything that was magical, and only this very moment in time mattered and there was no one to criticise and condemn. She thought of Melidor and Julie, coming here on their wedding day, to take possession of this paradise. Yes, it must have been heaven!

The light came on, startling her, bringing her back to frowning reality. Thor stood in the doorway looking at her; Reyna knew that he was stripping from her the only garment she wore—his dressing-gown. He spoke softly, his voice like the caress of a warm summer breeze.

'What are you thinking . . . Reyna?'

She felt something rise in her throat as she struggled with her emotions. Danger of this kind was so exciting . . .

'Of Julie and Melidor,' she told him, vitally aware that the very words were an invitation. She saw his fine lips curve in a smile as she took another couple of steps that brought him thrillingly close.

'The honeymoon lovers who came to paradise.' He spoke in low yet vibrant tones; another step closed the small space that had remained between them. She thought: if he doesn't make love to me it will be wrong, somehow. Yes, wrong. For this night, this situation, this moment . . . these would never be quite the same again. They were made for love. Just as, eons of time past, the environment was just right for the first stirrings of life in the deep wide oceans of the world, so was this moment of enchantment just right for the rapture of physical love. 'You say you have no boy-friend . . .' Thor's cool clean breath was on her cheek. 'Did any man ever tell you how beautiful you are?'

Colour rose delicately in cheeks that had gone pale.

'No.' Reyna shook her head as she smiled with her eyes. 'No—nobody . . .' It was a lie, and he knew it.

'You really mean,' he said, 'that you wish no one had said it . . . until I did.'

She nodded this time, but could not speak. Gently she was drawn into Thor's strong arms, tenderly kissed and caressed.

'Do you really want that drink I promised you?' Whispered words whose meaning could not be denied. She tried to hesitate, but only her voice faltered as she said, huskily because of the tightness of emotion that had settled in her throat,

'No-no ... n-not really——' She was swung into his arms, carried like a small and fragile doll to the room where she was to sleep. The rose-glow added to the romance of the situation; the bed was soft to her back as Thor laid her down. He went away and she had time to think, to see tomorrow if she wished. But she cared nothing for tomorrow; it was a million years away. Thor returned wearing a black dressing-gown. He looked like Satan, she thought, yet her lovely lips parted invitingly.

He stood for a long while, gazing down into her face. His expression was unfathomable; Reyna felt suddenly that she ought to rise and flee ... because although there was admiration in his eyes, they held no trace of anything akin to love.

'You're an enticing little wretch,' he said, smilingly beginning to discard the dressing-gown.

Wretch? Why did it sound all wrong? It was as if he were sorry to admit it, but he just could not resist her charms. With a sudden leap into reality she forgot every romantic notion that had possessed her. This was madness! But thank heaven she had regained her sanity in time! With difficulty she rose to a sitting position on the bed, carefully wrapping the dressing-gown round her quivering body.

'You must go!' she cried, feeling exceedingly foolish but at the same time determined to hold on firmly to her resolution. 'Please go, Mr Granville—I want to sleep!'

'Sleep!' Thor threw back his head and laughed. 'My dear girl,' he went on with gentle irony, 'you've left it far too late to change your mind.'

The cord of his dressing-gown had been untied, but he held both ends in his long slender fingers. She looked at them, fascinated, and recalling how she had told herself that those hands could never be kind, and caressing, and comforting ... only cruel.

'I want to go to sleep!' Her voice sounded petulant even to her own ears. 'Go away!'

The lazy topaz eyes reflected the laughter that had so recently left his lips.

'What made you decide you didn't want to be Julie?' he asked with amused interest.

'Julie?'

'Come on,' he chided gently. 'You were imagining yourself as Julie—that child bride—and I was your Melidor.'

'No—no,' she protested, for the moment diverted. 'It wasn't that. I wasn't play-acting ...' Her voice failed as tears welled up in her eyes. 'You obviously don't understand how it is with a woman ...' Again her voice failed, this time on a tiny sob. She tried to get off the bed, but Thor barred her way. 'Let me go, please. I want to go back to the cabin.'

'And face that monstrous centipede?' He was laughing at her, yet, somehow, she sensed that he was trying to fathom out why she had changed her mind. 'No, my dear, you'll be far happier here with me. I won't hurt you, or hold it against you. Life is for living and this situation has proved too much for both of us—it was bound to, wasn't it?' Again the amusement; she thought that never in her life would she meet anyone as devastatingly attractive as Thor Granville, the man of whom Patch had said,

'... he has a temper inherited from the devil and he's derisive of women.' Patch had gone on to say that Thor Granville had his own unique logic regarding the place of women in the world—in the kitchen or the nursery.

The nursery ... Sheer terror took the colour from her cheeks. She told him again that she wanted to go back to the cabin, but he shook his head decisively.

'You've burned your boats, my dear,' he told her calmly.

'You can't lead a man on like that and get away with it. He paused a moment, still staring down at her. 'What are you scared of?' he wanted to know after a while.

'It—it isn't anything I can explain,' she began, brushing a tear from her cheek. 'I'm not—not what you think . . .'

The fine mouth curved in what might have been a sneer. 'What's the game?' he demanded, but gently. 'Trying to convince me that you're an old-fashioned girl?' Those satanic brows were raised admonishingly. 'Too late, my girl, as I've just said. Forget the act and give yourself over to the enjoyment of the moment——'

'No!' she cried fiercely, the tears welling up again. 'I'm not acting! I know I've misled you—I mean, it's only natural that you'd think I'm—I'm no good, but I am! I am, I tell you, so there!'

Silence, deep and profound, while Thor looked at her with the most odd expression in those topaz eyes of his, and while in Reyna's eyes the tears continued to come forth from the cloud behind them. They rolled inevitably down her cheeks and she lifted the corner of the coverlet to flick them away. The childlike action, coupled with the genuine distress in her face, seemed to have a strange effect on Thor. He frowned, as if in self-condemnation, and moved away from the bed, at the same time re-tying the girdle of his dressing-gown.

'I always said that women are unfathomable,' he murmured, very softly, as if to himself.

'I'm sorry.' Reyna looked at him selfconsciously.

'So am I——' He broke off and laughed. 'Good night, girl! Pleasant dreams!' His glance strayed to the door as he moved towards it. 'There isn't a lock, I'm afraid. But you're quite safe. That sleep you mentioned won't be disturbed—unless it's by Shah barking at his own shadow in the moonlight!'

Reyna sat and watched the door close, softly, almost

noiselessly. And she remained there for some considerable time, still intensely aware of his presence . . . just as though he were still in the room. Why had she changed her mind just because he had uttered that one word which seemed so incongruously out of place in the romantic situation?

She gave a deep sigh and, slipping off the bed, discarded the garment that had almost buried her, putting it over the back of a chair. She got into bed and drew up the cover, then snapped off the light. The window drapes were slightly apart, allowing the moonlight to shaft into the room, argent and pale against the soft yellow wood of the wardrobe doors.

Reyna nestled into the pillow. She still thought it was wrong, somehow, that Thor had not made love to her.

CHAPTER SEVEN

REYNA sat down at the breakfast table, marvelling at the easy manner in which she and Thor had, between them, prepared the meal. No mention of last night, merely the casual question from Thor as to how she had slept. Very well, she had returned, managing successfully to adopt the same casual attitude as he was adopting. That dramatic incident might never have occurred—and in fact, Reyna did wonder if, in the far future, she would begin to doubt that it had ever taken place at all, but had been something out of her imagination, born of the romantic setting of tropical island, moonlit lagoon, and a terrifically handsome man.

They ate bacon and eggs, chatting in a companionable way but without any sign of over-friendliness. Thor had taken *croissants* from the deep-freeze the night before and put them in the oven while the bacon was grilling. They were delicious, as was the steaming coffee—that really did give off the correct aroma, not like the 'mutilated, powdered stuff' of which Reyna's Aunt Saran spoke with such derision at times. The large window was wide open and the breeze filtered in from the sea via the palms and casuarinas and the flowering plants that flourished in tropical profusion in Thor's wonderful garden. The minah bird flitted past, calling, over and over again,

'My name's Susan!'

Gaily-coloured butterflies fluttered in and out of the flower borders; a brilliant Madagascar fody was a flash of fire as it flew past and into the lovely orchard flower tree which, originally, had been discovered in the teak forests of Burma. How these trees came to be established on the island of Surcoufe no one knew. Patch had mentioned them to Reyna when describing some of the lovely flora of the island, and he maintained that seeds had been brought over either in pirate ships or by wind and birds.

'More coffee?' Thor held the pot aloft as he asked the question. Reyna nodded.

'Yes, please. It's delicious.'

She saw his half-smile hovering momentarily and wondered if he were thinking of her usual breakfast—of fruit and water. Well, it wouldn't be for much longer, she thought. Soon she would be able to bring over what was necessary to make tea and coffee—and in fact to do some cooking if she so desired it.

After the meal was finished Reyna helped to clear away the dishes, which Thor stacked into the machine. Then she thanked him for the bed and went on her way, entering the cabin cautiously, wondering if the centipede could possibly be still there. She thought not. There were numerous cracks and openings through which it could have escaped. The huge space under the door, for one thing.

She went to the villa and worked on it for the whole day, meeting Thor on her return along the beach. His eyes wandered, and he frowned. It was plain even before he spoke that he was puzzled as to why she should be always looking grubby like this.

'Hello, Miss Chapman. What have you been doing with yourself today?'

She shrugged carelessly.

'Just—er—roaming about.'

'All by yourself ...' His voice trailed to an unfathomable stop. His lazy eyes came alive all at once. 'The treasure?' Half question, but more a statement. Reyna was elated. Why hadn't she herself thought of it before now? She pretended to be shamefaced as she replied,

'Well, it's as much mine as it is yours.'

'How do you know? It might be on my land.'

'Yes, but it was buried by Pirate Harper for him and his cousin. It was their loot, not the loot of only one of them.'

'Nevertheless, it would belong to the person on whose land it was found ... and I'm very sure, Miss Chapman, that it would be my land.'

That confidence again, that subtle something that seemed to say that the whole of the island belonged to him. Of course it did not, but Thor Granville did act as if he were the sole owner. Perhaps, she mused, it was merely to anger her.

'I feel,' she said, 'that whoever finds it should share it with the other.'

His eyes flickered.

'You would share it with me?'

'But of course!' It was a sincere exclamation and he nodded appreciatively. But he said nothing and for a space both he and Reyna stood watching Shah doing his acrobatics as a fisherman. A large fish, silver in the sunlight, was having a difficult time, jumping right out of the water and high into the air. The dog would leap, jaws open, but always he missed. In the distance, on the seaward side of the fringing reef, a shoal of flying fish rose like a flock of birds and sailed for an incredible distance before dropping into the water again. Reyna had been fascinated by these flying fish, owing to the length of time they were able to stay out of the water. Would they eventually evolve into birds, she wondered, just as other sea creatures had done over a period of millions of years?

'So you would share the treasure,' observed Thor at last. 'It's generous of you, I'm sure.'

Sarcasm? Reyna could not tell. It did not matter anyway. All that did matter was that, at last, she had an explanation for her appearance. Let him believe she was searching for the treasure; she had every right to do so, as long as she was on her own half of the island.

'I must go,' she said presently. 'I want to make sure that centipede isn't still in the cabin.'

'It won't be.'

'No, I don't think it will, but I intend to make sure. So I'll have to search well before it gets dark.' She looked up into his austere face, into an unmoving angular mask behind which was ... what? The man often appeared to be preoccupied; Reyna wondered what he was thinking about.

Thor called to Shah, who came at once, and shook himself vigorously, drenching Reyna's bare legs and her shorts.

'I'm sorry!' exclaimed Thor. 'Are you very wet?'

She only laughed.

'The cool shower was lovely!'

He looked speculatively at her; she had no idea just how attractive she looked, this despite the grime and sweat that gave evidence of hard work. There was a rare sweetness about her full mouth, a tender expression in her large, doe-like eyes, which was accentuated when she smiled, swiftly and appealingly. Something moved in Thor's throat ... a nerve pulsating out of control. And then his lips snapped together as if some mental vision had caused his anger to rise.

'I'd better let you go.' His voice had changed dramatically. It was brusque almost to the point of dislike. 'Good luck with the treasure.'

'Thanks.' She turned, his changed manner hurting abominably. And she realised that she was having a most difficult task in suppressing tears as, walking away, she heard him speak to Shah—in soft and almost gentle tones.

'Good boy. Come on, we'll give you some tasty meat for your dinner.'

Two days passed without her meeting Thor Granville again, days spent at the Creole villa, the living-room of which was beginning to take shape. The wooden floor and walls had been cleared of all growing things, and of the soil that had supported them. Of the two windows, one was broken, but the two pieces were still in place, and the other was as good as new once Reyna had cleaned it. A few repairs to the floor, a new replacement here and there on the walls, and this one room would be ready for decorating and polishing—for Reyna intended to have a gleaming wood floor with one or two attractive rugs to take away the bareness. Fitted carpets—even if she could afford them—would be totally out of place here.

She had found several 'treasures' while pottering about the garden. A spade had turned up—rusty and with the handle partly rotted away, but the implement had proved of untold value in clearing away the debris that had accumulated throughout the years of sad disuse. A fork had also come to light, and was used regularly when, tired of working in the house, Reyna would spend an hour or two dealing with the weeds in the garden. She had cleared the path, which was of worn flagstones, and led to another path, still overgrown, which in turn led to the beach. Her own private beach! Reyna wished her aunt were here, helping her, enjoying the discoveries, revelling in the idea of spending her holidays here every year. Aunt Saran's job was that of clerk in the Education Department at County Hall; she had a month's holiday in summer or autumn and ten days at Christmas. Wouldn't it be wonderful to come here for Christmas? thought Reyna. Perhaps that would be possible; she must discuss it with Aunt Saran when she got back home.

Meanwhile, Reyna worked with a will, determined to have part of the villa ready for occupation before she returned to England at the end of her six weeks' vacation. She had brought ample money to spend, and this, in the form of travellers' cheques, she had deposited with the receptionist at the hotel, who had put it in the safe. Reyna meant to spend some of that money to buy the immediate necessities for her little house; these would all be brought back when she returned for her second visit. But she had to make sure first that she could change her flight, putting it off for another month.

Dusk was falling rapidly when at last she was making her way along the beach to her cabin, her rucksack heavy with the fruit she had picked for her evening meal and for her breakfast in the morning. How still the sea was! With nothing but the white spray of surf on the top of the reef. And the silence as she walked along the shore—an all-pervading, imperishable silence deeper than the hush of eternity. She stopped and glanced up. The moon had risen in the soft translucent sky even though the sun, a fiery sphere hanging close to the horizon, had not yet gone down. She felt alone, isolated from the world, and yet she was not lonely. She wondered what Thor Granville was doing at this moment. He seemed to disappear at times, but of course he must be around somewhere.

The following morning, though, when she went to his house for water, she became conscious of a strange prickling sensation running along her spine; it brought up the golden hairs on her forearms, and brought a moment of chill to her senses. She was at the sink, with the jug under the running tap. The back door had been closed, but she had turned the handle to open it, as instructed to do by Thor Granville when first he had offered to let her use his tap. Why should she feel like this? There had been other occasions exactly similar to this one, when she had come for water and there had been no sign of the owner of the house. She had concluded that he was taking the dog for a walk—or rather, walking out with the dog. Shah was one of those lucky ones who was loose all the time.

'It's not the same . . .' Reyna turned off the tap, and went from the kitchen as usual, but instead of closing the door she placed the jug of water on the step and went back into the room. She stood stock still, listening, her glance moving around, taking in the neatness, the total absence of a piece of crockery or cutlery either on the drainer or any of the Formica surfaces. 'No, it's not the same.' Always there had been Thor Granville's supper tray—over there on the end of that double unit. On a couple of occasions his breakfast things had been on the shining stainless steel drainer . . . This morning there was no sign of life at all.

Risking his annoyance, she called out. Nothing but a slight echo, and she shivered involuntarily. Only now did it come to her that the reason why she had never felt lonely, or afraid, was that always with her was the knowledge that Thor Granville was not too far away . . . the *comforting* knowledge.

Now she had no sensation of having him near, or even having his presence on the island at all! Yet, she argued, giving herself a mental shake, he must be on the island, simply because he could not leave any more than she could.

She called again, then went outside and called loudly, 'Shah!'

Something lodged in her throat; she was not of a nervous disposition, but there was something desolately frightening in this deep sense of being the sole occupant of the island.

'But I'm not the sole occupant. He must be somewhere about!'

At last she picked up the jug, but remained on the step, oddly reluctant to close the door behind her. And on impulse she put down the jug again and went through the kitchen into the room in which she and Thor Granville had dined the other night. Everything was in its place— not even a cushion disturbed or a book lying around. The smaller sitting-room was the same. She opened another door which led to the dining-room. The Sheraton dining table and matching chairs caught her eye, but she had no enthusiasm for the appreciation of art at the moment. She closed the door and turned back into the kitchen, that prickling feeling more pronounced as, bewildered, she began to visualise all sorts of probable and improbable explanations for this uncanny state of affairs. Naturally it had already occurred to her that he might still be in bed, but having gained a knowledge of his habits, she decided it was most unlikely that he was still asleep. Besides, where was Shah?

She stood irresolute; Shah might be off somewhere. Perhaps he slept outside, in which case he might be out in the lagoon trying to catch fish. And his master might just be lying in his bed, ill ... Most unlikely, but by no means impossible.

Reaching a decision at last, Reyna went into each bedroom in turn, choosing first the one she knew was Thor's. His bed was made, and a soft leather pyjama case lay upon it. A brush and comb on the dressing-table, a pair of sandals by the wardrobe door. On the cabinet by the bed were three books, one of which was *Palgrave's Golden Treasury*. There was a bedside lamp which matched the clock whose tick was the only sound in the deep unearthly hush pervading the room and the corridor outside it.

Reyna was in no doubt at all now that Thor Granville had not spent the night in his home. Where, then, had he spent it? Had he another house on a different part of his land? She shook her head, tossing away the idea as not feasible.

It was a mystery, and one that puzzled her greatly. If he was not on the island ...

'He must be on the island!' she said vehemently. 'He has no means of leaving it until the supply boat arrives.'

Forcing herself to put it out of her mind, she took up her jug and went off to her cabin where, after having her breakfast, she washed and changed, then went to the stream to wash her clothes, which she hung on a branch of a tree to dry.

The rest of the morning was spent as usual at the Creole house, but she was restless, and she was also conscious of her nerves being stretched, alert to every sound and movement. The bright plumage of a sunbird, iridescent in the sunlight, made her jump when the bird swooped down to settle briefly on a hibiscus flower, to probe the heart with its long beak. A short while later the noisy, querulous cry of a minah bird caused her to spin round, not knowing what she expected to see.

At half past twelve she looked at her watch and decided to go again to the Villa Surcoufe and see if Thor Granville was there. She had no excuse for going, but she was not troubled about that. She would explain, if he *was* there, that she'd been worried, as when she went to fill her water jug there was no sign of life.

She knew, even before she tapped on the door, that he had not returned.

She called, then wondered why. Without any doubt at all she knew that Thor Granville was not on the island.

Not knowing what she was looking for, Reyna turned her steps towards the far end of his gardens. She had not seen them before, as they were situated on a sort of triangle, the point of which was in effect the extreme eastern end of the island. She saw the beauty around her—the hibiscus and magnolia bushes, the lovely dome palms and the clustering bougainvillaeas beneath them, the pearly-white flowers of the climbing bauhinias—but little of it really registered. She had seen something through the trees, a structure which explained everything ...

A jetty. Thor Granville's private landing stage ...

Had he a yacht? He certainly had a boat of some kind; Reyna rather thought it would be a high-powered motor launch.

She inhaled in a deep, long-drawn breath. The hateful creature! He could have got her off this island any time he liked! His boat had been moored there, but she could not see it from anywhere on her own land. This place in his gardens was the only spot from which it would be visible except from the sea. Had she swum round to this point then she would have seen the jetty.

Where had he gone to? And did he leave yesterday or the day before? Reyna had not experienced that tingling sensation yesterday morning when she came for water. No, she rather thought that he had gone yesterday some time. To Victoria? She nodded, answering her own question. It was bound to be Victoria. And he could have taken her with him.

Slowly she retraced her steps, a dozen questions flitting through her mind. Had he done this deliberately so that she would be scared? Was it his way of driving her from the island? When would he return? He might not be intending to return until the supply boat had called and gone again, with Reyna on board.

The air was fresh and cool beneath the trees as she walked slowly back towards the house. The flowers sparkled in the garden, their exotic perfumes heady, pervasive. But the magic had flown; she was no longer at peace on the island, no longer enthralled with its isolation from the rest of the world, for there was fear in her veins and a deep sense of loneliness in her heart. Absurdly, she wanted to cry, while at the same time fully aware that tears would do nothing to relieve the ache left by the shock she had received.

Yes, undoubtedly it had come as a shock to her that Thor Granville could have acted in so callous a manner towards her. She was confessing unashamedly to herself that she was disappointed in him, that she hadn't wanted to discover a ruthlessness like this in his character. Much as she had taken to Patch she had come to realise that he had exaggerated a great deal regarding the way Thor Granville was supposed to have treated him. For one thing, Reyna could not imagine him driving the old man from his own property.

What an unpredictable man Thor Granville was, though! Reyna's mind flitted to that evening when she had dined with him; after he had said, in that stern decisive way, that the matter of her selling him her property would be shelved for the present, the evening had been as enjoyable as any Reyna had ever spent. He had walked her back to her cabin, a courtesy she had not expected but for which she had been grateful. He had excited her by admitting that he had enjoyed the evening. Then the episode of the centipede and its dramatic sequence when both he and she had stood poised on the knife-edge of temptation. Since that night she had recalled many times her admission that what she felt for Thor was the kind of emotion that could become most disturbing to her peace of mind—although the word 'love' had been ruthlessly rejected from her thoughts.

She sighed, and stopped by the lawn's edge, scarcely knowing what to do. This kind of a situation had never been visualised when on impulse she had decided to come over to the Seychelles. Her intention had been to stay at the hotel in the capital, on the island of Mahé, and sail over to Surcoufe each day, the idea being to impress Thor Granville that the island was not his alone, that she owned the other half and that she meant to visit it. Vaguely she had planned to harass him, to torment him by her threats to develop some of her own land, to build hotels and encourage tourism. In this way she felt sure she would be keeping faith with Patch. None of it had worked out, and now she was all alone on Surcoufe, and would be unable to leave for another five days.

A deep sadness assailed her and tears filled her eyes. She thought of her pleasure in the renovation of the little Creole villa, of her profound sense of peace as she proceeded with the all-absorbing, creative task she had set herself. And now it was no longer exciting, because she was feeling so lonely and lost. Lonely and lost, owing to the knowledge that Thor Granville was not on the island ...

She remained very still and silent, standing beneath a mango tree russet with blossom ... and it was when her heart contracted painfully that she reluctantly admitted to having fallen irrevocably in love with the man she had come here prepared to hate.

Dawn shafted through the darkness, pearl-grey and mauve, then soft translucent amber. Reyna had lain awake for hours, and had risen while it was still dark, opening the cabin door because the heat was stifling. She had washed and dressed by the light of the torch, then had her breakfast. Listlessly she reached for the jug which she had returned to the shelf, and went along to the villa for water. The lagoon, draped with a coverlet of orange and rose, lay unmoving in the flaring sunrise, while away beyond the reef fishermen were out in their boats, the sails swinging in the breeze. A truly magical morning, but Reyna found it impossible to shake off her depression. This loneliness was too much; the sense of total isolation carried with it a vague fear—not of anything on the island, but of such things as accidents. Supposing she fell and received an injury, or what if she were suddenly taken ill? Her thoughts naturally drifted to Thor Granville and his callousness in not offering to take her to Victoria, but the next moment she was admitting that it was in no way incumbent on him to offer her help; she was nothing to him—except a nuisance, of course, a hindrance to any plans he might have in mind regarding the island's fate.

As soon as she entered the grounds of the Villa Surcoufe she realised that its owner had returned. Shah was sniffing round, exploring a flower border. He saw her and wagged his tail, but that was all; he made no attempt to come to her. It was amazing how her spirits had lifted on seeing him, and her step was light as she approached the back door. It was closed and she knocked before turning the handle. There was a woman at the sink; she turned her head as the door swung inwards.

'Oh . . .' Reyna stared in surprise. 'I—er—usually come to fill my water jug.'

The woman, of African extraction, smiled and moved away from the sink.

'Mr Granville said you would be coming. Miss Chapman, isn't it?'

'Yes, that's right.' Reyna put the jug under the tap. She was curious about the woman, who seemed quite at home in the villa. However, she merely filled her jug and carried it to the door. 'Thank you very much,' she smiled, turning her head.

'You're the young lady who's come over from England?'

Reyna nodded, realising that the woman was just as curious about her.

'I own half of Surcoufe,' she said, resting the jug on the step.

'Own half——' The woman shook her head. 'How can you own half of Surcoufe? It belongs to Mr Granville. Everybody knows that.'

Reyna stiffened, her eyes glinting. So he had told everyone that he was the owner of the whole island, had he?

'Can I ask who you mean by everybody?'

'People he knows on Mahé; I come from there,' the woman went on to elucidate. 'Victoria. I come over when Mr Granville wants me, to clean through and to do the garden. I sleep in that shed over there.' She thumbed towards the window, indicating an area of dense tropical vegetation.

'I didn't know there was a shed over there. How often do you come?' inquired Reyna, wondering where Thor Granville was at this moment. Obviously he wasn't about, as the woman would not be gossiping if he could overhear her.

'When he wants me,' said the woman again. 'Sometimes he sends for me to come on the supply boat and sometimes he brings me with him when he returns to Surcoufe after attending to his business.'

Reyna's eyes flickered with interest.

'He has a business on Mahé?'

'He owns several hotels. Two of them are on Beau Vallon Beach—the Pomerac and the Cordia; another is on the island of Praslin.'

Hotels ... It seemed very likely that he wanted to develop Surcoufe.

'You say he sends for you. How can he do that?'

The woman looked surprised by the question.

'He has a radio telephone here. He would have to, wouldn't he, so as to keep in touch with the managers of his hotels?'

'A radio telephone ...' So he could have had any of the pleasure boats pick her up and take her off the island. It was obvious that he had not wanted her to leave; no, he wanted her to stay and be thoroughly uncomfortable in the cabin—so uncomfortable that she would never have come back once she had left. 'How long are you staying this time?'

'Until all the work is done. I might go back on the supply boat, but if not Mr Granville will telephone for *La Belle Coralline* to pick me up and take me back to Victoria.' The woman had returned to the sink, where she appeared to be softening a window leather ready for use.

'Did you come last night?' asked Reyna.

'Yes; it was very late. Mr Granville was at the dinner-dance at the Pomerac. His lady-love was there,' added the woman with a swift, spreading grin that revealed a row of even white teeth and one gold filling.

'His——!' Reyna stared disbelievingly. 'He has a girl-friend?'

'Oh, yes! He's ...' Her voice trailed off and she turned swiftly to her task. Reyna, glancing towards the far door, noticed Thor standing there, his face an expressionless mask. It was impossible to tell whether or not he had heard what was being said.

'Good morning, Miss Chapman,' he said coolly, his glance flickering over her indifferently. 'How are you?'

'Fine, thanks.' She turned, picked up the water jug and left without another word.

A girl-friend ... How very strange to learn this! He had said himself that he had no interest in women. Perhaps he had meant that he had no interest in marrying one of them. She herself had thought that, being so attractive as he was, it would be almost impossible to accept that he had not had at least one love affair in his life. Well, it was plain that he was having one now.

After placing the jug of water on the shelf she ventured forth again, and even in her present state of dejection the wonders around her could not be ignored. The sun, rising higher above the horizon, had vanquished the last lingering shades of dawn as it sprayed the forest trees with rose and gold-quartz. Within the confines of the reef the painted lagoon lay still and glass-smooth, while on the white sandy shore the palms and casuarinas quivered tremulously against the sky.

The little Creole villa was cool and shady, nestling as it did within the shelter of its trees—date palms and flamboyants, a lovely Flame of the Forest and a stately tamarind with its dense crown of feathery leaves.

As she entered the living-room Reyna glanced around in brooding silence at her handiwork. It was incredible what she had been able to do in so short a time, and with nothing more than the few implements she had salvaged from various parts of the garden and from the room which had obviously been the kitchen when Julia and Melidor lived here. She wondered what Thor Granville would think of the transformation when eventually he saw it, as of course he must see it.

She gave a deep sigh, recalling her first sight of the villa, which had been almost hidden by the vegetation smothering its walls and windows—vegetation which had, for the most part, acted as a preservative. She had felt the first stirring of a new experience, the excitement of adventure as on impulse she tore away some of the weeds or loosened the grip of some tenacious creeper. With a stab of dejection she turned away, to stand in the garden where, in her mind's eye, she had seen a smooth velvety lawn, exotic flower borders and maybe, one day in the far distant future, a little fountain, its water electrically driven.

Suddenly she stiffened. Voices!—one of which was a woman's. Had Thor Granville brought his girl-friend back with him?

'But, Thor, if it's as you say then why don't you act in your customary dictatorial and high-handed way and tell her to sell—or else!'

Reyna froze. The voice was smooth and silky, faintly censorious as it voiced the words 'dictatorial' and 'high-handed', but itself imperious as the final words were uttered. It was obvious that the girl disliked Thor Granville's masterful ways, but at the same time she supported him in his desire to get his hands on the whole of the island.

'It's a difficult situation,' returned Thor exasperatedly. 'Like every other woman I've ever met she's obstinate without knowing why!'

Reyna's eyes glinted with anger. Obstinate, was she, just because she refused to pander to his wishes and sell him her property! The girl's voice was heard again; she was coming closer, or so it seemed, and Reyna glanced round automatically for somewhere more secluded in which she could conceal herself. She went back into the house, into the part she had not yet touched, and crouched down among a tangle of ferns and wild raspberries and lavender sorrel.

'... think we're all obstinate, darling. Have you ever found me ... obstinate?' The voice purred over the last few words. Their subtle meaning was simple for Reyna to grasp. Thor Granville laughed and said with a hint of mocking satire,

'You, my dear Celia, are talking about pleasure; I'm interested in *business* at the moment.'

The girl laughed, softly, huskily.

'You're a strange one, Thor. I'm beginning to think I ought to have married you. Life would never have palled.'

'You had the chance.' The reminder was spoken lightly, but Reyna, her ears alert and keyed to catch any further subtleties, was strongly of the opinion that, whatever the reason why this girl Celia had not married him, Thor Granville had been deeply hurt at the time. He had got over it, though, and now the two were friends again. Not an unusual occurrence between lovers, but somehow not to be associated with a man like Thor Granville. Reyna would not have expected him to be of the forgiving kind.

'And now ... have I the chance again?'

Reyna felt her breath catch as she waited for his answer. None came. Instead, he changed the subject, asking her how long she could stay on Surcoufe.

'For as long as you want me, darling,' she purred in response. Thor Granville laughed without humour. Yet his voice was throaty and sensuous as he rejoined,

'I expect then, my love, that it will be for at least a week.'

'A week ...' Low the tones and huskily enticing. 'A week on this Robinson Crusoe island. How did you ever find it, Thor?'

'How did you ever find it ...' The words were turning over in Reyna's mind. Again this implication that the whole of the island belonged to him. How had this girl got the idea? From Thor—or from the gossip which seemed to be going on about him on the island of Mahé where, it would seem, he was fairly well known?

'By keeping a look-out,' he answered, and now his voice held a hint of boredom. 'Do you suppose you'll enjoy being here, away from civilisation, for a week?'

'With you, Thor, I could stay here for ever.'

'Charming,' he returned with sarcasm. 'I'm profoundly flattered, my dear.'

'Hateful creature! I'm glad I threw you over!'

'Yet you wouldn't, had you your time to come over again.' A statement, firm and tinged with triumph—malicious triumph. Pompous, self-conceited creature! The girl must have no pride at all to tolerate being spoken to like that!

'And yet,' mused Celia, 'I don't know if I could have taken your domination without resistance.'

'Resistance would have brought its own punishment.'

'Too well I know it! Your temper's something I never want to see again as long as I live!' No answer from Thor Granville. Celia went on after a while, 'Your wife, Thor, would have to be totally without spirit. You'd have to be displaying your mastery the whole time.'

'You're probably right, my dear.'

'I know I'm right! You do well to remain a bachelor.'

'Again you're probably right. Come on, if we're intending to go for that swim then we ought to be turning back.'

'We've been walking for over an hour—and on your land the whole time! What does it feel like, Thor, to be lord of all you survey?'

The couple were walking away. Reyna missed Thor Granville's answer, but her blood was boiling anyway. Lord of all he surveyed indeed! That was *her land* they were on! Reyna became furious with herself for not going out there and ordering them both off, informing them that, far from being the lord of all he surveyed, Thor Granville was trespassing!

CHAPTER EIGHT

IT was less than three hours later that Reyna came face to face with Thor Granville's girl-friend. Unable to concentrate on her work at the villa, Reyna had decided to take a stroll along the beach—her beach. And sauntering towards her as she swung round a small bluff and came into a cove of powdery white sand was a tall, assured girl, dark-haired and slender, with perfectly-formed features and large, attractive brown eyes, eyes which swept with interest over Reyna before gleaming with a sort of amused contempt. Reyna coloured, painfully aware of her grubby appearance—the dusty jeans, the blouse that could no longer be described as white, since the only washing it ever received was in the cold water of the stream, and with the scant lather provided by the toilet soap which Thor had given her. Her shoes, of the sandal type but a little more robust, were now fit only for use in the garden.

Celia, on the other hand, was beautifully turned out in a sun-suit consisting of shorts and sun-top, with a matching full-length beach skirt split right up the front from hem to waist. It was in a most attractive shade of salmon pink with white trimmings and large, corded buttons down one side of the skirt, the same cord having been used for the corresponding buttonholes on the opposite side of the skirt. The girl's hair was long and sleek, and she wore a pair of large white earrings in the shape of stars. Certainly a glamorous and exceedingly attractive girl, admitted Reyna, her heart like lead as she thought of her own feelings for Thor Granville. Even had all else been equal she could never have stood a chance against a girl as alluring as this.

'Hello.' Celia was the first to break the silence that had

127

fallen as the two girls stopped and stared at one another. 'Miss Chapman, I believe? My name's Celia Markham. Thor told me about you.' The dark eyes moved again, to make another examination of Reyna's figure. 'You look as if you've been working?' she observed, a curious inflection in her tone.

Reyna drew a breath. She had not expected to meet the girl, or Thor Granville either, as it was not often he came on to her part of the island. Something urged her to say, without making any effort to be friendly,

'I don't know if you're aware of it, Miss Markham, but you're trespassing. This beach is on my property.' She pointed to the stream some way ahead, which ran into the sea. 'Mr Granville's land, at this particular point, ends on the far side of that little rivulet.'

While she was speaking the girl's eyebrows had lifted, and her lips had curved in the sort of amused smile that was bound to infuriate Reyna, even without the supercilious words that came later.

'Indeed? Thor hasn't mentioned anything about my not being allowed to cross that delightful little rustic bridge which, I believe, was erected by him.'

'He had no right to erect it. I expect the reason why he did so was because, as there was no one else living on the island, he came to regard it all as his own property. However,' persevered Reyna in face of the look of amused disdain in the other girl's eyes, 'its presence there doesn't give him, or any of his friends, the right to trespass on my land.'

'I'll tell Thor what you've said,' laughed the girl. 'I daresay he'll be very amused.'

Reyna's eyes sparkled dangerously.

'Amused or not,' she retorted sharply, 'he will not in future come on to my land! And now please go back. I don't want you here on this beach!'

She supposed she felt antagonistic against the girl simply

because she was Thor Granville's friend ... more than a friend, obviously. Thinking about her conversation with the woman who had come to clean for Thor Granville, Reyna did not doubt that she was about to say—when prevented by the unexpected appearance of her employer —that he had brought his girl-friend back with him to Surcoufe.

'You're ordering me from this beach?' Arrogance now in Celia's voice, and a glint in her eyes as forbidding as any Reyna had seen in those of Thor Granville. 'I would have a care if I were you, Miss Chapman. Mr Granville is not the man to be dictated to by a woman.'

'I scarcely think it could be called dictatorship. I'm within my rights in forbidding either you or anyone else to come on to my private property.'

'Within your rights, eh?' drawled Celia. 'Oh, well, it isn't my quarrel,' she added with a careless shrug of her shoulders. 'I expect Thor will sort you out in the end.' And with that the girl swung around and went back the way she had come.

Reyna stared at her, her mind filled with strange misgivings. On several previous occasions she had felt twinges of uneasiness, vaguely suspecting that all was not as it appeared on the surface. She had already gained the impression that Thor Granville held all the aces, and could play them just whenever it suited him to do so.

The girl had used strange unfathomable words.

'I expect Thor will sort you out in the end.' Obviously Celia knew something ... but what? The more Reyna brooded on the matter the more complex the situation became. She felt convinced now that Thor Granville did have the whip hand, but further than that she could not see. Nor was she intending to dwell on it any longer. She would continue to work on the villa; it not only gave her something to do, but it was infinitely rewarding as well.

She was on her way back to the cabin at dusk when the

woman she had been speaking to approached her carrying a canvas shopping bag over her arm.

'Hello,' Reyna greeted her, smiling. The woman was on
her land, but Reyna somehow did not resent her presence
in the way she had resented Celia's.

'Hello, Miss Chapman.' The woman hesitated a moment
and then, 'My daughter makes dresses and sells them on
the market, mainly to tourists. They're embroidered— '
She opened the bag and withdrew an evening dress of
white cotton, heavily embroidered round the hem and on
the wide, stiffened belt. The top was perfectly plain with
a slashed neckline, the front and back being held together
on the shoulders by bows of the same material. Reyna's
eyes widened; the dress was beautiful, though rather
creased with having been folded in the bag, and at a
glance it appeared to be just the right size.

'You're selling it?' asked Reyna unnecessarily, and the
woman nodded eagerly.

'When Mr Granville said there was a young lady living
on Surcoufe I thought it would not do any harm if I
brought a couple of my daughter's dresses along.'

'You have another?' Reyna's eyes went to the bag, but
she was already holding the white dress against her. Even
the length appeared to be right.

'Yes, but seeing your colouring, I think it won't do.
She lifted part of the dress and Reyna immediately shook
her head. She never wore pink.

'How much is this one?' she asked, wondering if she
had enough money with her. If not, she would pay the
woman a deposit and give her the rest when she got back
to Victoria.

'It is not expensive, Miss Chapman.' The woman told
her the price and, satisfied, Reyna said she would try it on.

'It will fit,' said the woman, happy to be making a sale.
'I'll leave it with you and come for the money tomorrow
morning.'

Reyna shook her head.

'I'll try it on at once, and pay you now—if it fits, that is.'

She would have been very disappointed if it had not fitted, as it was so beautifully made, and most reasonably priced.

'I'll wait, then.'

Reyna went into the cabin and tried on the dress, washing her hands and face first. It fitted to perfection and, thrilled, she paid for it, handing the money to the woman who was standing at the door nodding her head in admiration.

'It's just right for you, Miss Chapman. Your friends at home will envy you this lovely dress.'

'I don't doubt it,' agreed Reyna, fingering the embroidery of the belt. 'Your daughter is very clever.'

'I think so too. Thank you for buying the dress. Goodbye, Miss Chapman.' The woman walked briskly away, to disappear into the tangled vegetation of the forest.

For the next two days Reyna was constantly expecting Thor Granville to approach her with some cutting comment on the order she had given his girl-friend. So when eventually she did encounter him she braced herself for the verbal battle she was expecting to have with him. It came as a shock, therefore, to hear him say in pleasant, almost friendly tones,

'I wonder if you would care to dine with me again this evening, Miss Chapman? You've already met my very good friend, Miss Markham, and there'll be another guest, Richard Gieves. He'll be arriving on Surcoufe later today.'

Reyna thought of his meanness in not taking her into Victoria, then instantly told herself again that it was not incumbent on him to offer her a passage. She wondered how this other man was going to arrive here. Had he also got a boat of his own? Thor Granville was staring fixedly at Reyna's soiled blouse and asked amusedly if she had been searching for the treasure again. She nodded her head and said yes, she had been looking for the treasure, and hoped she had injected sufficient curtness into her voice to put him off asking any further questions.

'I don't know about this evening,' she began, her mind seeing an intimate dinner-party where she was the guest of the man she loved but did not trust, and he was giving all his attention to the girl whom he had once loved and whom he had wanted to marry. The other man seemed unimportant; Reyna was not even curious about him.

'I understand how you feel about clothes,' Thor Granville was saying. 'But I've already put this to my friend and she's willing to lend you a dress——'

'I have one, thank you,' broke in Reyna tersely.

'You have one?' in some puzzlement.

'Your cleaning lady sells them. I bought one from her.'

He nodded his head, the hint of a smile curving his lips.

'She knew you were here and would naturally bring some of her daughter's work with her. She's always got an eye to business,' he added with a brief laugh. Reyna, staring up into his handsome face, saw the austerity leave it for a few seconds and caught her breath. How Celia could have thrown him over was something that Reyna could not understand. Even his arrogance, his imperious manner, seemed unimportant. It would be worth all the mastery and domination to see him soften like this now and then. He was talking again, saying that as Ouma was there to wait on the table it would be a little more civilised than last time. Reyna could have said that it was very civilised last time, but she refrained, saying instead, as she played for time while she made up her mind whether or not to accept his invitation,

'Ouma is the woman who sold me the dress?'

He nodded.

'Yes; she comes here regularly to work in the house and

the garden.' He paused a moment. 'You'll come?' he said at length. 'To make the foursome?'

She ought to resist, Reyna told herself, for it could not possibly be as pleasant as that other evening, when she and Thor Granville dined alone. Yet she wanted to dine at his house again, wanted to be in his company. It was all very illogical, she knew, but found herself accepting his invitation for all that.

'Thank you for asking me,' she added, unable to keep her mind off the more practical aspect of the matter—that of eating her fill of good solid food!

'I'm glad you're coming,' he returned and, looking up into his face, Reyna knew that he spoke the truth. 'And you don't want the loan of a dress?'

'No, but . . .'

'Yes?'

'I'd be grateful if I could iron my dress.'

'Give it to Ouma; she'll be delighted to do it for you.'

'Thank you.'

'About half-past seven—but come earlier if you want.'

He left her, striding away in the twilight, an impressive figure even in his shorts and checked shirt, open at the throat and with the sleeves rolled up to the elbows. As masculine as any man could be, thought Reyna, and a sudden bleakness enveloped her at the idea of her being so foolish as to fall in love with such a man. Good-looking he might be, but beneath the veneer he was an avaricious man to whom money was all-important in life.

Two hours later she was tapping at the back door of the Villa Surcoufe. Ouma opened it, her big brown eyes widening to saucer dimensions.

'Oh, but you look very beautiful!' she exclaimed, bringing a rosy flush to Reyna's cheeks. 'You haven't seen yourself, because you have no mirror in that cabin, so go through to the hall first and take a look! Wait until I tell my Gaata how lovely her dress was on you——!' Ouma

broke off, turning as Thor Granville appeared in the doorway across the room. 'Mr Granville, have you ever seen a
picture like this! My daughter——'

'Yes, Ouma,' broke in Thor Granville suavely, beckon-
ing to Reyna for her to come in. She entered and for a
long profound moment stood there, vitally conscious of
those strange eyes upon her, taking everything in, from
her shining hair—which she had washed only that morning—to her face, its colour that pearly amber that is the
beginning of a beautiful tan. Her cheeks were flushed,
glowing with health, her lips rosy and invitingly feminine.
She saw his eyes move almost imperceptibly to her dress,
which she knew full well accentuated her curves. Thor
broke the silence at last, saying softly, as if he were not intending his voice to carry into the sitting-room,

'A very charming dress, Ouma. It certainly looks delightful on Miss Chapman.'

'Thank you, Mr Granville,' murmured Reyna, endeavouring to maintain her composure in face of the admiration she saw in Thor Granville's eyes.

'Come in and meet my friend,' he invited, and the next
moment she was feeling the strength of the handclasp as
Richard Gieves looked down at her and said he was
charmed to meet her. He had hazel eyes and fair hair and
a slow attractive smile which gave a homely aspect to his
round, good-natured face. Celia, whose critical eyes had
taken in all that Thor's eyes had taken in, appeared to be
frowning beneath the pleasantry of saying that she was
happy to be meeting Reyna again.

Drinks were served; Reyna, alert as always when in
Thor's company, felt she was not imagining things when
she suspected Richard and Thor of exchanging significant
glances after their eyes had flickered to her as she sat on
the sofa, her back against the red velvet upholstery, the
embroidered skirt of her dress spread out like a huge fan
at her feet.

'Thor tells me you're staying on Surcoufe.' Richard's voice was low and cultured, his eyes fringed with lashes any girl would envy. Reyna, conscious of Thor's interest, and the fixed stare of Celia, answered shyly, wondering if Richard knew what her accommodation was like. She had the impression that Thor had talked about her at some length with his friend. 'How's England? It's almost two years since I was home.'

'You work here?' Reyna bypassed his question as she put one of her own.

'I'm Entertainments Manager at one of——' He stopped abruptly as his eye caught that of his friend. Then he went on talking, his face a mask, telling Reyna that he worked at an hotel, that his job was interesting, that he had worked in South Africa before coming to the Seychelles. Reyna showed polite interest, but with a flash of imagination she saw him at one of Thor Granville's hotels, knew for sure the reason why he had cut his words at a sign from his friend. Celia inserted a few words into the conversation and after a while Richard said, when Reyna had addressed him as Mr Gieves several times,

'Can't we be a little more friendly? What's your name –besides Miss Chapman?'

'Reyna,' she answered shyly.

'Can I use it?'

'Of course.'

'Good! We'll all use our given names, eh, Thor?'

He nodded carelessly, his glance flickering to Reyna for a second.

'As you say, Dick, it's a little more friendly.'

Reyna gave a small start. Thor's eyes had come to hers again and there was no mistaking the admiration in them, and the friendliness. She knew a sudden warmth, a pleasant emotion that affected her heart and pulse and nerves.

Celia alone seemed not to be pleased with the idea of using first names, but Reyna knew in any case that she could not address the girl as anything other than the formal 'Miss Markham.' She was too unfriendly, though Reyna could not really blame her, not after she had been ordered off Reyna's land.

The dinner was a great success, the table being lit by candles in silver holders, and at each cover Ouma had put small flower decorations. The food was delicious, the wine of the best quality. When the dinner was over they all went from the dining-room to the sitting-room where Ouma served coffee and Chartreuse.

The conversation flowed, but somehow Reyna was not one hundred per cent comfortable. She sensed something in the atmosphere that was beyond the scope of words to described. Celia's attitude she could understand. It merely reflected her own, there being no love lost between them and therefore any exchange of words between them was merely the civility incumbent on them as guests in Thor Granville's house.

But it was Richard's attitude that brought a tinge of uneasiness to Reyna, since he himself seemed more than a little uncomfortable. And he seemed to have a guilt complex for some reason or another.

Thor was the charming host, but even he seemed to frown inwardly now and then, as if at some unpleasant thought that had entered his head. In spite of this, though, he did send an admiring glance now and then in Reyna's direction. Celia missed nothing and several times Reyna saw the girl's eyes narrow in an expression of dislike.

'I think it's time I was going.' Reyna felt actually relieved when the time came for her to utter these words.

'I'll walk with you,' from Thor as he glanced at the clock. And then he added, with the merest hint of humour, 'Let's hope there aren't any centipedes in the cabin to frighten you tonight!'

Reyna managed to laugh, totally unprepared for what was to follow as a result of Thor's remark.

'Centipedes?' echoed Celia with a slight shudder. 'Those massive things they have on Mahé? Do you have them here as well?'

Thor nodded lightly.

'Reyna had one on her bed.'

Celia frowned as she transferred her gaze from Thor to Reyna.

'What on earth did you do?'

'Did you manage to kill it?' asked Richard with interest.

'No, it disappeared. I ran out of the cabin, you see, and when I went back it wasn't there.'

'Did you sleep knowing that horrid beast was in your cabin?'

'Reyna had to stay here,' Thor enlightened Celia casually. 'I happened to turn round—I'd walked her back to the cabin and——'

'Walked her back to the cabin?' Celia's interruption was sharp and brittle; her eyes slid coldly towards Reyna who, having half risen in preparation to leave, had sat down again.

'Reyna had dined with me,' said Thor calmly. 'Naturally I walked back with her. It was after I left that, turning, I noticed she was outside, with the torch. I turned and went back, to find that she'd seen this centipede.'

'She'd dined with you . . .' The girl seemed to be talking to herself, seemed to have forgotten completely the presence of others in the room. 'And you walked her back to that cabin.' Celia leant forward to where her cigarette case lay open on the table by her chair. Languidly she took out a cigarette, leaning towards Richard as he flicked a lighter. Through the flame her eyes met Reyna's, narrowed eyes, and maliciously dark beneath perfectly-arched brows. Reyna felt a tingle run along her spine, an icy chill of inexplicable foreboding. 'And then she stayed here.' The girl's voice had changed to a curious, dry echo of what it was. 'Stayed the night?'

Thor was frowning heavily.

'That's what I said.' His tone was short but not harsh, but beneath it Reyna sensed a deep and arrogant fury. She felt sure that, once he found himself alone with Celia, his whole manner would change and she would be given the dressing-down she deserved. As for her own feelings—Reyna had never been more uncomfortable, more anxious to be alone.

'I must go,' she said, glancing at Thor. 'It's all right, I can go alone. You mustn't leave your guests.' She had risen, feeling awkward, conscious of Celia's hostile gaze, and Richard's unfathomable one. Probably he, like Celia, was putting some construction of his own on the fact that she had stayed in the villa all night.

'I'll come with you,' responded Thor firmly. 'If you'll excuse me——?' His glance embraced them both. 'I'll not be long.'

'There really isn't any need,' began Reyna, when she was interrupted by the raising of Thor's hand.

'Tell me,' purred Celia, whose lips had curved un-expectedly in a smile, 'how big was this centipede, Thor?'

'I didn't see it.' His voice was short, betraying impatience at what he considered to be an unnecessary question. But Reyna with her swift woman's intuition knew just why the question had been put. Celia now knew that Thor had not seen the centipede, and she was suspecting Reyna of making the whole thing up ... so that Thor would take her into his home for the night. Anger surged within Reyna, and the look she shot at Celia was as malicious as any the girl had shot at her this evening. She said, her voice edged with ice,

'I assure you, Miss Markham, that there really was a centipede, no matter what you might be thinking to the contrary,' and with that she turned away angrily, and it was only as she reached the door that she remembered her manners and turned to say good night to Richard.

The stroll to the cabin was a silent one, with Reyna feeling miserable because of what Thor must be thinking about her rudeness. He would not understand, being a man, the kind of tenseness that had grown up between the two women. Such things went over men's heads, being, to them, the sort of trivia which only females would indulge in.

It was as they came in sight of the cabin that Thor said,

'I hope you enjoyed the evening, Reyna.'

She caught the tinge of doubt in his tone and said without thinking,

'It wasn't as enjoyable as——' And then she stopped, putting a hand to her mouth. 'Oh, I'm sorry——'

'No need to be,' he broke in with a hint of grim humour. 'I'm flattered that you found that other evening so enjoyable. It was more ... intimate and cosy. Is that what you meant?'

She glanced up, slanting him a glance of suspicion.

'Are you being sarcastic?' she asked tersely.

'Not at all. I'm serious.'

'I don't understand you at all,' she told him complainingly.

'I believe you've said something of the kind before.'

They were nearing the cabin and through a gap in the thick forest vegetation the calm indigo waters of the lagoon lay dreaming beneath the fleecy, starlit sky.

'Sometimes you make me think that—that ...' To put her thoughts into words was not easy. But Thor seemed perceptive and said in his quiet, finely-timbred voice,

'That I'm not quite so sinister as your good friend Harper asserted?'

'It wasn't sinister,' she was quick to deny. 'Nothing quite as bad as that.'

Thor laughed, and Reyna, suddenly realising that this

situation was in fact humorous, responded to his laughter.

And it was at this moment that she felt every muscle tighten at a sound that caught her ears ... the unmistakable snapping of a dry and lifeless twig beneath someone's foot ...

She swung round automatically, her eyes peering into the darkness and seeing only the drift of stars through the gently swaying branches of the trees. She looked up at Thor; he seemed not to have heard anything, because he was saying, with scarcely a pause,

'Villainous, then. Is that how your friend described me?' Reyna brought her full attention back to him.

'I must admit that he called you a rogue.'

Again Thor laughed. Reyna felt her heart jerk in a thrilling, exciting way. The man was far too attractive when he laughed like that! It was youthful laughter, the kind that made you feel about sixteen and ready to take his hand and dance away into the land of make-believe. She looked around. This *was* the land of make-believe, a magic, unreal island where only dreams existed.

'A rogue, eh? Poor chap, how little he knew. Maybe I ought to have acted differently ...' His voice trailed away to silence and Reyna was left wondering if he really was sorry for the way he had treated poor old Patch. What an unfathomable man he was! She glanced up to read his expression, but saw only a set profile in the dim light from the night sky. She knew, though, that even if she had been able to see his face it would have been an expressionless mask.

'I'll say good night, and thank you for the marvellous meal.' Her voice betrayed nothing of her feelings—the puzzlement she felt but, more so, the responsiveness to the magic all around her.

If Thor had taken her in his arms she would not have wanted to resist; if he had bent to take her lips she would have given them gladly.

To love a man yet not trust him. It seemed impossible. Perhaps she could trust him ... yes, she was beginning to think that, if only she knew everything, she most certainly would find that he could be trusted.

The following morning she was walking along the beach when a voice hailed her and she turned, a swift frown of annoyance creasing her forehead. Celia, clad in a gay towelling beach robe, was strolling leisurely in her direction. Reyna stopped, waiting for her to come up.

'I'm glad I've seen you,' was the first thing the girl said, as if she would forestall Reyna, should she be thinking of ordering her off her land again. 'I just want a few words with you, Miss Chapman. I shan't keep you long.'

Reyna's frown deepened. There was nothing she wanted to hear from the girl, but she made some attempt at civility as she said,

'You want to talk to me? Is it important?'

The girl smiled faintly; that she was amused was obvious.

'I think you'll be interested,' she answered with confidence. She glanced around. 'Shall we go into the little copse there? It's more private than here.'

Reyna lifted her eyebrows.

'Private? How much privacy do you want? There isn't anyone——'

'Thor and Richard are out somewhere. I'd rather not have Thor know that I've been talking to you.' No embarrassment in Celia's manner, just the cold hauteur that seemed to be a permanent part of her make-up.

'Very well,' returned Reyna briefly, and went towards the shelter of the bushes.

'It's about Thor and me,' began Celia without preamble as, following Reyna, she entered the shady copse and turned towards her. 'I think you ought to know that he and I are very much more than friends, that we've known each other for several years ... and that we're soon to be married. I tell you this for your own good, Miss Chapman, since it was very obvious to me last evening that you've fallen in love with Thor and so——'

'I have not fallen in love with Thor!' snapped Reyna, hoping the lie sounded more convincing to Celia's ears than it did to her own. 'What an absurd assumption you seem to have made!'

'Have I?' slowly and pityingly. 'My dear girl, it was as plain to see as that reef out there, and if Thor couldn't see it too then he's far less perceptive than he usually is.'

Reyna went hot all over. How could she have given herself away like that? Suddenly she wanted to run away, to leave Surcoufe for ever, and never set eyes on either Thor or Celia again as long as she lived.

'Is—is that all you have to say?' she was able to get out at last. 'If so, then please leave me.'

'You're embarrassed, naturally——' Celia broke off and shrugged lightly. It was plain to Reyna that the girl was enjoying herself immensely, happy in the knowledge that she was inflicting mental pain as well as causing deep humiliation. 'It was unbelievably foolish of you to fall for a man like Thor. He's a man of the world, a man of culture and taste and an aristocratic background. He'd never even look seriously at a plain little schoolteacher who's never——'

'Schoolteacher!' broke in Reyna, catching her breath. 'How do you know I'm a schoolteacher?'

'Thor told me.'

'Thor ...' Reyna shook her head bewilderedly. 'Thor told you?'

'He made it his business to know who it was that had come into——' Celia stopped and frowned as if she were not quite sure of the way in which she ought to be phrasing her word. Eventually she shrugged and carried on, 'into Mr Harper's property. He employed a firm of solicitors in England to investigate you, to find out all about your job, and what sort of person you were.'

So Thor had known all along that she was a working girl ... Many things were explained now, thought Reyna, her one clear recollection being Thor's comments when she had been talking about the formation of the reef. He had guessed that she had studied geology at some depth. But to think that he had had the impudence to have her 'investigated'! And then to keep silent, allowing her to make every kind of fool of herself—and laughing at her all the time she was doing it! Reyna felt at this moment that she actually hated him, felt that it was as well he wasn't here, as she must surely have told him exactly what she thought of him. Her embarrassment increased, consuming her as she pictured Thor talking to his girl-friend, telling her all this, and then they would both have laughed together—

'I hate him!' whispered Reyna to herself, and she meant it. 'He's the most detestable creature that ever lived! Poor old Patch was right after all, and I was wrong in thinking he'd exaggerated about the man he accused of being a rogue!'

'I don't think there's anything more to say, Miss Chapman.' Celia's voice was low and still amused. 'Perhaps I should say this, though—if you have any self-respect you'll leave this island without any further delay. The supply boat comes in a day or two, as you know ...'

Reyna never moved as the girl drifted away, disappearing like a wraith as she made for the shore. What must she do? wondered Reyna. To go away was the easiest course, but everything that was strong within her rebelled at leaving Thor Granville in sole occupation of Surcoufe. And more than this, she had an obligation to Patch, whose object in giving her his half of the island was to prevent Thor from having it. Then there was the Creole villa: somehow Reyna had come to feel she owed it to that couple to renovate their little house, to bring it to life again, so that the spirits of Julie and Melidor would never really die. It was all very dreamlike and romantic, but Reyna was a dreamer and a romantic and she would never be ashamed of admitting it.

She moved at last, lifting her head to the breeze as she made her way to the villa. It would take more than Thor Granville and his girl-friend put together to make her leave her self-appointed task unfinished!

'I'd be a coward to leave what I've begun, just because of those two,' she mused as she came in sight of the villa, a little mellowed building looking picturesque among the trees. Her thoughts wandered on and she was remembering that sound she had heard last night. Could it have been Celia? The girl could easily have followed them, having told Richard that she was going into the garden for a breath of fresh air. Yes, decided Reyna, it *was* Celia she had heard. And so the girl must have heard them—Thor and herself—laughing together. Was Celia jealous? Reyna shook her head, trying to dismiss the idea, but it persisted. For if Celia were jealous then it would explain her attitude towards Reyna ... explain why she had spoken as she had, and advised Reyna to leave the island.

CHAPTER NINE

On her arrival in Victoria Reyna went straight to the airline offices and to her satisfaction she was able to change her flight. The date she chose was a month hence, giving her two days at home before the new school term began.

Then she embarked on a shopping spree after first having changed all her travellers' cheques at the bank. She bought some good pieces of secondhand furniture, some hand-made rugs from the market in Victoria and curtains from a shop selling ready-mades and also the materials. Reyna bought enough matching materials to make cushion covers and, in the case of her bedroom, a counterpane. Kitchen effects included a butane stove with a small oven, a large water tank and a pail to fill it from the stream. A few dozen candles were included, but there were two lamps as well, which used the gas. Reyna learned that the bottled gas was supplied regularly to Thor Granville and she gave her order to the same firm. By chance she met an English girl in a small café where she had gone for her lunch and they got into conversation. The girl, Alma, fair-haired, blue-eyed and vivacious, asked outright what she was doing here.

'You don't look as if you're on holiday,' she added, casting a significant glance at the stack of parcels which Reyna had put on the floor beside her chair.

'No,' she smiled, 'I'm not on holiday altogether.'

Altogether?' Alma's eyes held an interrogating expression. Reyna could not resist telling her about the island, so charming was the girl's manner, so spontaneous her curiosity.

'So you're doing this house up,' commented Alma when Reyna had finished speaking. 'What a nice thought on your part to renovate it. But there must be a dreadful lot of hard work?'

'There is,' returned Reyna with a grimace. 'The trouble's been that I had nothing to work with—nothing really useful, that is.' She went on to add that she *had* found one or two useful implements after a time, and this made the work much easier than it had been at first.

'And now you've been buying some more, by the look of it.'

Reyna nodded, smiling.

'I've had a wonderful time,' she confessed. 'I've bought some furniture—including a bed and wardrobe, so I shall be moving into the villa once it arrives.'

'They'll be on the suppy boat next Wednesday?'

'Yes, but I'll be back on Surcoufe before then. I've booked to go on Saturday on *La Belle Coralline*.' Reyna eventually asked Alma where she was working, guessing almost immediately that she lived permanently on the island of Mahé.

'I work in the Land Registry Office here, in Victoria,' Alma answered.

'That sounds interesting. How did you come to get a job like that? I mean, don't they usually have their own people whenever possible?'

'I came with my brother, who's a surveyor. He got me the job last year when our mother died and I had no one left in England. Fred's the fatherly type and felt I oughtn't to be living on my own, unprotected——' She broke off, her eyes twinkling with laughter. 'He became very forceful about my joining him, but he had no need to be. I didn't really need any persuading to come to the Seychelles to live.'

'You're lucky,' commented Reyna, then went on to explain her plan for coming out to Surcoufe each summer for the whole six weeks of her vacation. 'And I hope to come at Easter and Christmas as well,' she added. 'My aunt might come with me on some of these occasions,' she ended.

'I think it's a super idea. Surcoufe's one of the loveliest islands in the Seychelles. I know someone who's been there once or twice, before Mr Granville went to live there. He stopped the boats calling; everyone was sorry, but I suppose you can't blame him for wanting his privacy. I believe he's built a fantastic house there?'

'Yes, it's very attractive indeed.'

Alma was looking at her watch.

'I'll have to be going. Look, why don't you come to our flat this evening—come for a meal. Fred'll like to meet you.'

'Well . . .'

'I expect I've made him formidable, saying he's fatherly and forceful, but he's quite human really. Do come.'

'All right—and thank you for asking me.'

Alma was already writing the address; she passed the paper across the table and at the same time began to explain how to get to the flat, which was at a place called Hermitage, just south of the capital.

Reyna went as promised, and thoroughly enjoyed the evening. Fred was quiet, studious, but friendly for all that. Alma was talkative, full of life, and Reyna came away feeling she had made two friends. She thought she would invite them over once the villa was ready and she had moved in. Fred might not want to come, but Reyna felt sure that Alma would accept the invitation. She could come on a Saturday and arrange for one of the tourist boats to pick her up later, or even pick her up on the Sunday.

Alma had talked a little about her work and Reyna had learned that her own name would soon be on the Register, as the owner of half of the island of Surcoufe.

It was mid-morning when *La Belle Coralline* drew close to the island and Reyna prepared to get off. As before she had rolled up her jeans, but this time she had several bulky packages with her in addition to her two large suitcases. A

couple of young men helped her, though, and soon she was
on the shore, her possessions around her, waving to the
tourists standing by the rail. She had checked out of the
hotel that morning, being fortunate enough to extend her
stay three days longer than the period originally booked by
the travel agent in England.

There was no sign of Thor, and for this she was thankful.
She would have been flustered and uneasy in his presence,
thinking about Celia's assertion that he had guessed that
she was in love with him.

While she had been in Victoria she had endeavoured to
put his face out of her mental vision, but had failed. It was
an undoubted fact that he dominated her thoughts; he was
there when she went to sleep and there again when she
awoke. In view of this it was the height of stupidity
even to think of returning to Surcoufe. Go home, her
common sense urged. Put a few thousand miles between
you. The distance will take his attractions out of focus. But
instead of listening to these wise and warning murmurings
of her mind she continued with her plans for a return to the
island and the complete renovation of the part of the villa
on which she had made a start. She would soon be cured
of her feelings for him when he was married to Celia . . or
would she?

A sigh escaped her and she tried not to think of Celia
as his wife, and in the end she had almost convinced herself that the girl had been lying when she claimed that
they would be married soon. For there had been nothing
of the lover about Thor on that evening when Reyna had
dined with him and his two other guests, one of whom was
Celia. Nor had he revealed any emotion during the conversation which Reyna had overheard. On the contrary,
he had seemed quite cynical towards the girl, his voice betraying a sort of malicious triumph when he had said that
Celia would now change her mind about marrying him, had
she her time to come over again.

Reyna began carrying her packages to the cabin, and from there she took a few things over to the villa. Thor was no longer occupying her thoughts, as her activities left no room for anything but the excitement of the project in hand. Armed now with implements and utensils which made her task so much easier, she began to make rapid progress, and it was not until the Monday that she realised she was again alone on the island.

How long had Thor been away? She had a feeling that he was not on the island when she landed last Saturday, but she could not be sure. Nor did it trouble her in the least; she had no sensation of that aloneness which had troubled her on the first occasion, no feeling of fear or even trepidation. In fact, it suited her that he should be away, since there was no chance of his discovering her activities at the villa.

And to her great satisfaction he had not returned by the time the supply boat came along with all her purchases. She stood on the shore watching the furniture being unloaded and carried ashore by two men wading in the lagoon. Then came the rugs and bedding, and the large cardboard boxes in which she had carefully packed her crockery and glassware, and one or two ornaments, cheap but by no means gaudy. They would help to make the place look like home until she could afford something more tasteful. Time and time again the two men went back to the supply boat, bringing the gas cylinder, the butane stove, the large water tank, a tall cardboard box containing a broom and a polishing mop, tins of furniture polish, scouring powder and much more besides until at last everything was unloaded and placed on the shore.

Reyna had to smile, thinking that this was surely the most unusual 'removal' that had ever taken place. It would be something to tell her colleagues when she got back to school next month. The men obligingly took the things to the villa; they were two Creoles, one with tight woolly curls that were almost as light in colour as her own hair. She gave them a tip, thanked them for helping her, and came back to the shore to watch the departure of the supply boat. By this time she was really excited, and for the rest of the day Thor Granville scarcely entered her thoughts at all.

By the following afternoon the living-room and bedroom were a delight to Reyna's eyes. The floors, their holes rather amateurishly repaired by the very simple nailing on of new pieces of wood which had come with the rest of her purchases, were polished and the rugs laid over the repairs. On the walls Reyna had hung a couple of 'tapestries' she had bought in the market at Victoria, and a small brass-framed mirror which though a little spotted by damp was, she felt sure, a genuine antique. Most of the furniture was second-hand, the sideboard beautifully made from Saman wood—the wood of the raintree. This same wood had been used for the floor and interior walls of the villa. It was known for its durability and for the beautiful finish that could be achieved on it. There was a table and two chairs, a little side table on which Reyna placed one of the ornaments. She had bought a set of shelves in basketware and these she fixed in a corner of the room, and on the shelves she had placed little pots of flowers fashioned from coconut fibre.

'I think that Julie and Melidor would approve,' Reyna mused happily. 'It's not too bad at all for a beginning.'

She had managed to find a woman in Victoria who was willing to come over once a fortnight with the supply boat and see that everything was in order at the villa. As the supply boat usually stayed close to Surcoufe for about an hour and a half, the woman would have ample time to do what was required. A small wage had been agreed upon and there was of course the boat fare in addition. Reyna hoped to be here at Christmas, bringing her aunt with her.

She was dying to show her the villa, and the half of the island she owned.

She had debated a long while on what she would call her little house. Julie and Melidor had not named it, apparently, because on the deeds it was merely marked as a Creole house. At last Reyna decided upon Villa Samana, since there was a beautiful specimen of this spreading, canopied tree in the side garden. Its other names—in addition to raintree—were cow tamarind and monkeypod. It was said to be the most symmetrical tree in the world and its flowers were delicate pink tufts rather like miniature brushes. Reyna had heard a legend about it from someone in the hotel. It was supposed to produce rain at night, and according to this ancient story, it 'rained from the branches the juice of the cicadas'.

Although Reyna was sceptical about this rain, she could not ignore the fact that the grass beneath the tree was more lush and green than anywhere else in the garden!

Having satisfied herself that the house was ready to move into, she brought over the rest of her things including her two suitcases of clothes, leaving the cabin exactly as she found it. She had managed to secure the door of the villa, having fixed the new hinges she had bought, but there was no proper lock—just a bolt which she could use from the inside. She was humming happily to herself as she hung up her dresses in the wardrobe and put the other things into the chest of drawers. A white rug at the side of the bed and another in front of the dressing-table was all she had by way of floor covering, but as she had managed to bring up the original polish on the wood she was quite contented with the result. She had 'fringed' the material used for the bed cover and that looked most attractive—much nicer than a hem, she thought, her glance going to the curtains which, of course, matched the cover.

Her food was stored in the cupboard she had bought for the kitchen; she had tinned and packet vegetables and soups, tinned meat and fish, and several cartons of long-life milk. What a boon modern science was! She was short of nothing except fresh bread—but she did have packet toast.

After filling her water container from the stream, and a smaller one with drinking water she had fetched from Thor's house, Reyna decided to relax for a few days, taking advantage of the sun, the sea and the lovely walks which the island had to offer. She had several good books and a small tape recorder, all of which she had brought with her from England, so she could never be bored even if it rained.

It was while she was strolling along the beach that she saw Shah at his extraordinary game of chasing fish in the lagoon. So Thor had returned. He came into view presently; Reyna had on a pretty sunsuit consisting of shorts and a brief top in pale blue nylon trimmed with white, and she saw his eyes widen long before he reached her. She had by now acquired a most attractive tan which made an arresting contrast to her hair, especially at the temples where it had been bleached to silver by the sun.

'Hello, Reyna,' he greeted her, his glance going to her hands, which were no longer roughened by hard work as she had not done any for four days and in addition she had treated them with a very excellent hand-cream. 'So you're back.'

'Yes,' briefly, and then, with an upward glance at him, 'If—if you'll excuse me ...' She felt embarrassed, which was only natural, since all that Celia had said came flooding into her mind—the fact that Thor had known all the time that she was a working girl and, even more embarrassing, the fact that he probably knew that she had fallen in love with him.

'You want to run off?' His perceptive eyes took in her

flushed cheeks, the quivering movement of her lips. 'What's wrong?'

'Nothing——'

'Then why do you want to run away?'

She made an impatient gesture.

'I can please myself, can't I?' she said pettishly.

His brows lifted in surprise, as well they might, as the last occasion on which he was in her company they had parted on the friendliest of terms.

'You don't appear to be in the best of tempers,' he observed rather sternly. 'Had enough of your own company? Is that it?'

'I love my own company!'

Thor regarded her in silence for a space, his brows knitted in a frown.

'You'd better come over and dine with me this evening,' he said at last and on a distinctly imperious note. 'It's plain that you *are* fed up with your own company, no matter how much you might deny it.'

She looked at him, desire weaving its way through caution and preventing the swift refusal that ought to have come in response to his invitation. To dine with him again ... alone ... Yes, it must be alone, because he hadn't made any mention of anyone else. Besides, she had heard him say that he would want Celia to stay with him for a week, and that was much longer than a week ago. To dine with him alone ... The words repeated themselves over and over again, though she was not fully conscious of the fact.

'I don't know——' she began, when she was cut short by an imperious lift of his hand.

'Come early, then you can help me prepare the meal.'

'I didn't say I'd come,' she said. But, immediately impelled by curiosity, she added, 'I don't know why you should be so concerned about me—about my being alone, I mean?'

To her surprise the smile that touched his lips was almost tender. However, all he said was,

'My dear girl, I'm merely being neighbourly.' He glanced at his watch. 'I shall expect you in a couple of hours—around seven o'clock.'

Reyna found herself nodding and murmuring huskily,

'I'll be there—and—and thank you for inviting me.'

What was the matter with her? she was asking herself a few minutes later as she entered the villa. Where was her pride?

And yet, she realised, if she had not heard what Celia had to say, then she wouldn't be feeling like this, nor would she even have contemplated refusing Thor's invitation to dinner.

'I shall forget all she told me! I'll just act as if I don't know anything about Thor's having me investigated. And as for his having guessed that I've fallen in love with him—well, I'm not sure of that anyway, so why should I allow it to trouble me?'

And with that she felt much better, and by the time she was ready to go to the Villa Surcoufe she felt happier than at any time since that very first dinner with him, when it had all been so cosy and romantic.

The dress she wore was in white cotton with bright yellow flowers printed upon it, and sprays of green leaves. It was a bold design, and very attractive. The neckline was high but the back slit to the waist. The bodice fitted snugly to her curves, while the skirt, gathered tightly at the waist, was full and flowing, with a ruched frill forming the hem. Sleeveless, it revealed her lovely sloping shoulders and slender arms and accentuated the tan she had acquired while sitting in her garden, the garden of the Villa Samana, as she had now come to think of her house.

Such an unusual address: Villa Samana, Surcoufe, Seychelles.

At exactly seven o'clock Reyna was knocking on Thor Granville's back door; as before he was cooking, but this time she was by no means as ravenously hungry as on the first occasion. Her meals were now exciting to prepare and appetising to eat. Thank heaven for such things as canned meats and dehydrated vegetables, she would think as she stood over her butane stove preparing her lunch or evening meal.

'Ah, there you are, right on time.' Thor smiled as he beckoned her inside. He closed the door and then turned, his lazy topaz eyes flickering over her from her gleaming silver-gold hair to her dainty white sandals and her perfectly-manicured toes peeping through, just an inch below the frilled hemline of her dress.

She coloured and glanced away, shy and unsure of herself as she wondered what he was thinking. Perhaps it had not struck him that she now had all her clothes with her, so the dress and sandals were a complete surprise to him.

The silence stretched, broken only by the faint ticking of a clock on the wall. What was he thinking? Reyna asked herself again. Could it be that he was interested in her? Breathlessly she held on to the idea, and, quite suddenly, it seemed not so remote a possibility after all. His glance, his manner, the smile that hovered on his lips—faintly mocking, it was true, as was the expression in his eyes, but it was a sort of amused mockery, as if he would have been happy to tease her in some way. Yes, undoubtedly his whole attitude was that of a man who has found his companion interesting. His next words not only added to the impression, but strengthened it.

'You look charming, Reyna. That dress is most attractive.'

'Thank you, Thor.'

He laughed softly, and the corners of his eyes crinkled in the most attractive way. Vitally aware of him, of the magnetism that seemed to emanate from him, Reyna could only stand there, looking up into those amused eyes, her own held because he willed them to be. It was only when her lips twisted into a strained expression that he withdrew his mastery, and laughed again.

'You're shy,' he murmured softly. 'So refreshingly shy.' Reyna's lashes fluttered down; she said nothing, but waited breathlessly for him to speak again. 'Go into the sitting-room,' he said. 'I'll be with you in a moment or two.'

The spell was broken; her feeling of relief was strangely mingled with one of disappointment. She said, glancing at the stove,

'Can't I help you? You said I could.'

'So I did, but I can't run the risk of your soiling that dress.' He shook his head decisively. 'There isn't much to do—merely to put the finishing touches to one or two things.' His tone was a firm dismissal; Reyna went immediately to the sitting-room, into an atmosphere of soft lights and quiet music, with the delicate perfume of flowers being wafted through the air by the fan revolving from its pendant in the ceiling. Through the window the scene was of a purple night with a star-spangled sky above a smooth metallic-dark sea where, on the horizon, the lights of a ship twinkled as if vying with the stars.

Caught in the magic of her surroundings, Reyna brought her dreamy gaze back to the room, and the table, where crystal glass sparkled against the less scintillating glow of smooth old English silver.

She turned slowly as Thor entered, his tall frame most impressive in an off-white tropical suit, loose-fitting and casual, designed to afford maximum coolness and comfort in a hot climate. His shirt was cream, his tie black but embroidered in gold and silver thread. Reyna knew it was Italian, and very exclusive; she had seen similar ties on sale in Venice. He stood looking at her, a half-smile on his lips. She caught her breath, her heart skipping a beat. His smile deepened, and he shook his head slightly, as if unable to understand that any woman could be so shy these days.

They had their drinks, then dined in the seductive atmo
sphere of flower-scents and classical music and the copper-
orange glow from the tall candles set in silver candelabra
at each end of the table. The dinner was superb, the main
course consisting of Creole food—an enormous fish cooked
in spices and sprinkled with chopped onions and other
garnishes; the vegetables were green peas and sweet
potatoes, with individual side dishes of crisp noodles and
rice. For dessert there was fresh fruit salad and whipped
cream, both of which had been brought over that morning
from Victoria, along with the fish.

When the meal was over they went out on to the
verandah, where they drank their steaming coffee in the
heady perfumed coolness of evening. Reyna knew again all
the magic of that other occasion when she and Thor had
dined alone—the sensuous delight, the awareness of
heightened emotions plucking at heart and nerves, the
sensation of exquisite fear and excitement. But there was
one important difference between that first occasion and
this one: she was now in love with the man in whose house
she was dining ...

All through the meal she had been conscious of a tension
within her, as if she were expecting Thor to say something
that would change her whole life. He had talked, but would
often fall silent, preoccupied, and a mask would slide over
his features. It was as if he were in the grip of some
mental struggle—accepting, rejecting, over and over again.
Accepting and rejecting ... what?

Now, as they sat on the verandah, his glance strayed to
her as, for a moment, Reyna stared at him with a puzzled
expression in her eyes. She saw a sudden coldness touch
his features; it seemed to be a rebuff, because she was staring at him like that—a rebuff that was so achingly notice-
able that an actual physical pain throbbed close to her
heart. She glanced down, wondering if the rest of the evening was going to fall flat simply because she had allowed

her excitement and expectation to soar to impossible
heights. But all at once Thor seemed to realise how she
was feeling and he smiled at her reassuringly. Her heart
lifted.

'More coffee?' he asked, and she nodded and smiled and
said yes, she would like another cup. And then, on an
impulse she could not control,

'You're a surprising person, Thor,' she said.

'Because I enjoy cooking?' There was a challenge in his
voice, as if he dared her to suggest that cooking was not a
manly kind of hobby.

Reyna caught the challenge and answered guardedly,

'I can see why you enjoy it; I do myself. But you've
always struck me as the kind of man who would expect the
kitchen to be the woman's province.'

Thor gave a brief laugh.

'I wonder what our friend Harper told you about me?'
he said.

Reyna fell silent, naturally, her eyes wandering to the
shore, where the plumy foliage of the palm trees made grey-
green shadows on the smooth white sand.

'Are you a good cook?' asked Thor, changing the subject when he saw that she was not going to be drawn into
answering his question.

'Not very,' she admitted, 'but I like experimenting.'

'You entertain, when you're at home?'

'A little, but it's rather expensive these days——' She
stopped abruptly, but soon added, on a note of resignation,
'I'm only a working girl, but you've already guessed that.'

Thor looked at her, an odd expression in his eyes.

'What makes you say a thing like that?' he demanded
sharply.

She bit her lip, searching for a plausible answer.

'Well, you—you spoke about my knowledge regarding
the reef.'

'Yes?'

'And you said that I wouldn't have studied coral reefs without studying some other aspects of nature—er—if you remember?'

'I remember very clearly.'

'I believe you knew at that time that I was a—a—schoolteacher.'

'You do?' with a faint lift of his eyebrows. 'And I was so perceptive that I could make an accurate guess at your occupation?' Reyna made no answer and after a short, considering moment Thor added, 'I'd have to be more than perceptive; I'd need to be omniscient.' Still no word from Reyna. She merely waited, expecting him to pursue the matter and she was already searching her mind for some feasible answer to the question she felt sure he would put to her. However, to her amazement he asked her outright if she had been speaking with Celia. Reyna's visible start was sufficient answer and he nodded thoughtfully.

'I saw her going along the beach and assumed she had called to you because you turned around. I didn't see any more because Richard and I were engaged on something more important.' He stopped rather abruptly and an inexplicable frown settled between his eyes for an instant. Reyna had the impression that whatever he and Richard had been engaged upon was now causing him some annoyance. 'I suppose she told you I'd made it my business to find out something about the person to whom Harper had left his property.' So casual, the way he spoke of his 'investigating' her! He might almost have had the right to know all about her! 'Tell me,' went on Thor curiously, 'just what did Celia say to you?'

'Nothing much at all,' Reyna said prevaricatingly.

'You feel you must shield her? Most commendable, my dear. I shan't embarrass you any further. We'll change the subject. How long are you proposing to stay here?' The question came so smoothly that Reyna failed to catch the strange inflection that had edged his voice.

For another two weeks.'

I see . . .' He became thoughtful, but there was nothing to be read from his expression. Reyna glanced down, her attention arrested by the dog; he was chasing some nocturnal creature which had been unfortunate enough to catch his eye. Reyna watched him race across the lawn and on to the beach, then he was lost to her vision. But her glance continued to rove, scanning the distant horizon where the pewter-dark sea met the star-filled arc of the heavens. The moonlight, pure and immense as the bounds of infinity, sprayed the sea and reef and the silent waters of the lagoon with silver. The moon itself seemed close to the earth, flaunting its grandeur over the tiny island, an island uninhabited but for the two people sitting there, on the verandah above the scented garden.

Out of the deep silence Thor's voice came softly to Reyna's ears and she looked at him, a smile on her lips.

'You look very happy,' he observed. 'Is there some special reason?'

'No, not really . . .' But she *was* happy, there was no doubt about that. Perhaps it was because of Thor, and the way he was treating her, but on the other hand it could be her sense of achievement at rescuing the little Creole villa and making it habitable again after all these years. One day she would effect the improvements which her mind visualised. It was an aim—and everyone should have an aim in life.

'Not really, eh?' Thor spoke gently, the shadow of a smile on his face. 'You're a strange girl, Reyna, but a very attractive one——' He stopped because of the start she gave and the rise of colour in her cheeks that tinted them so delicately. A nerve pulsated in his throat and it seemed for a space that he was lost for words. But then he looked at his watch, gave a small sigh and said, 'It's time I took you home, my dear. Come, we'll walk along the beach.'

It was not very late, but Reyna felt sure that Thor had

realised that temptation would affect them both again if she stayed much longer. Did he love her? The question came again and again as they strolled along the silent beach. Thor left her at the cabin door; she waited until he had gone out of view, then moved on through the forest, where thin shafts of moonlight piercing the foliage of the trees lit her way to the Villa Samana. She entered and put a match to one of the lamps, then stood looking around. Ought she to have told Thor about the villa? He would have to know very soon—in fact, she was rather surprised that her activities had not been discovered before now. Obviously he had not come close enough to notice any difference in the immediate surroundings of the villa—the openness of the garden area now that she had cut down so much of the undergrowth, the cleared paths, one to the beach and one to the stream. She had fixed a little iron gate she found buried in the soil, and painted it white. On it she had fixed the name of the house, written in paint on a piece of wood.

She closed the door and shot the bolt. She hoped Thor would like her little home, and not look on it with disdain, because it was so inferior to his.

CHAPTER TEN

REYNA allowed her eyes to make a full circle as she swung her slender body around with the ease and grace of a ballet dancer. A small sailing yacht in the distance—travelling to the island of Praslin, probably—its red sails brilliant in the sunshine; the shimmering water breaking in lacy white wavelets over the coral reef; a tiny wooded islet drowsing in the lagoon ... all this and a canopy of sapphire sky as well, clear and brittle as glass in the fierce light from a tropical sun. Reyna had risen early, had her breakfast on the verandah, tidied up the house, and now she was on her own beautiful beach—where the exquisite little bay was shaded with palms and takamakas waving gently in the breeze.

A deep sigh escaped her as she stood there, in shorts and a sun-top, gazing from one idyllic scene to another. It was too much! How could she possibly leave it all and return to the routine of school with its fixed working hours? She thought of the autumn which would be almost there when term began, the autumn drifting into winter days of mist and frost and long dark nights when all one could do was shut away the dismal scene outside and settle down with a book. Yet until now she had never found anything wrong with such a life. Her days were interesting, her evenings welcome after the strain of dealing with Jimmy Lloyd and his kind. Children were great fun, but wearing. They demanded your attention for every minute they were in the classroom and in consequence the long lonely winter evenings were a boon rather than a hardship.

But now ... To have known another life, to have sampled the delights of a tropical island, to own an enchanting little villa ... and then to be forced to leave it all ...

Her thoughts were interrupted by the appearance of Shah. She heard him splashing and turned to see him chasing a huge fish that writhed and twisted, in and out of the water, in order to escape the snapping jaws of the dog. Reyna laughed as Thor came striding along, forgetting that he was on her land until he said,

'Good morning, Reyna. Mind if I trespass? I haven't been along here for months. Very pretty——' He looked at her briefly before glancing around, then brought his eyes to her face again.

'I don't mind at all,' she answered, smiling. She did wish her heart would behave normally, and not beat so fast as it was doing. She wondered, in a flash of exquisite vision, what it would be like to be married to him. Would your heart turn a somersault like this every time you were in his company? she asked herself. Not very comfortable—but certainly exciting.

'You're a long way from your cabin,' he commented. 'You must have been up early.'

'I was.' She paused; it was on the tip of her tongue to tell him about the villa. She found she wanted to show it to him, to have his congratulations on her handiwork, and the result achieved. But before she had time to make up her mind he was speaking again, saying that he was going over to Mahé and asking her if she would care for the sail.

She looked at him, startled by his offer but excited by it too, and with no thought of not accepting it.

'I shall be returning this evening, but it will be late,' he added. 'I have some business to do in Victoria.'

'I'd love to come with you,' she said.

'You can find something to do?'

'Yes, of course.' She would probably be able to see Alma in the café. Then in the afternoon she would roam around Victoria, visiting the market and the shopping area, buying some of those things which she had put on her shopping

list and which she never expected to bring back to Surcoufe
until she returned at Christmas—or even at Easter, since
she was not by any means sure that she would have the
funds with which to have another visit so soon after this
one. 'Are you going right away?'

'In about half an hour.'

'Shall I come to your house?' She glanced down at her
shorts. 'I'll have to change first.'

Thor nodded.

'Yes, come along to my house. Try not to be more than
half an hour. I've an appointment to keep.'

He called to the dog and they went off. Reyna waited
until Thor was out of sight before making her way back
to the villa, which was completely hidden both by the
trees on the shore and those in and around the orchard.

Promptly she arrived at his house, clad in cool blue cotton
and sandals to match. Thor's appreciative eyes swept over
her, taking in the plain style of the sun-dress, the good
quality sandals and handbag, the wide-brimmed hat which
she carried. She looked very young, and felt it. She thought
of Thor's age—Patch had said he was thirty-five—and in
a flash of mental deduction realised that he was twelve years
older than she.

The yacht, motor-powered, was the last thing in luxury.
Reyna stood for a while beside Thor, watching his expert
handling of the vessel. But after a time she left him to
stand by the rail at the other end, fascinated by the great
shoals of flying fish as they glided out of the water, and
across it, like a flock of seabirds. They appeared to be just
as at ease out of water as in it, travelling their incredible
distances through the air before gliding back on to the
water.

Thor was silent, even when she joined him again; she
had the impression that he had something very important to
attend to in Victoria, and could not help wondering just
how hard he did work. From the first it had amazed her that

he could just live on Surcoufe, content to do nothing. This was the impression she had gained from what Patch had told her. Now, however, she knew that, if he owned these hotels on Beau Vallon Beach, then he must be a very busy man.

He turned at last and spoke to her, asking if she was enjoying the sail.

'I love it!' she answered enthusiastically. 'What more could anyone want than to be sailing on this calm sea, with the sun shining and these enchanting islands scattered all over it?'

He smiled then, as if releasing something from his mind.

'You're a romantic,' he said with a hint of amusement. 'I always pictured schoolteachers as sharp-featured people who'd become a little soured by shouldering the burden of other people's children.'

She laughed, a tinkling, silvery little laugh that brought an odd, unfathomable expression to his carved brown features.

'Were your teachers like that?' she asked.

'I seem to remember that they wore a pinched, weary sort of look, and I had the impression that they were living for the day when they would retire and try to forget that there were such things as those tormenting little brats they used to teach.'

Reyna laughed again.

'I don't know if I believe you,' she said. 'I expect you got on very well with your teachers—that they liked you and you liked them.'

'Oh, I didn't dislike them. I felt sorry for them.' He regarded her with a critical stare. 'It would appear that changes have occurred, and that the teaching profession isn't such a bad one after all. It certainly hasn't done you any harm.'

She coloured daintily, realising, not without a sense of surprise, that she was experiencing no embarrassment at this conversation. She ought to have been, though, seeing that she had tried to deceive Thor, making him believe she was a wealthy young woman who could afford to spend a fortune on developing her half of the island.

'Thank you,' she returned demurely. 'I'm happy in my job, you see.'

'That's obvious.' A strange hesitation and then, 'Could you settle on Surcoufe, do you think?'

'Settle?' What did he mean? wondered Reyna, her heart turning a somersault again. 'I—I——' She coughed nervously and turned away from his disconcerting gaze. 'Perhaps ... but not until I retire ...'

It was Thor's turn to laugh.

'In forty years' time, eh?'

She said nothing. His voice, edged with humour, seemed at the same time to be totally impersonal, and his whole attention had returned to his steering of the boat. Mahé was there, coming closer rapidly, and soon Reyna was on dry land, arranging to be back on the harbour at half-past nine that evening.

Alma was in the café when Reyna entered. She went over to the table, and pulled out the vacant chair.

'Hello!' Alma was delighted, but almost before Reyna was seated the smile disappeared and a slight frown touched Alma's brow. 'What are you doing here?'

'Mr Granville was coming over to Mahé on business and asked me if I'd like the sail. I'm meeting him at half-past nine this evening——'

'Mr Granville offered you a lift over here?'

'Yes ...' There was something very strange about Alma, decided Reyna. She appeared to be uneasy and uncertain, as if she had some unpleasant news to impart. This impression was soon to be proved correct, for when Reyna had ordered and the first course had arrived, Alma said suddenly,

'Reyna, that land on Surcoufe which you say you've inherited—is it really yours? I mean——' She stopped and considered, trying to be tactful. 'I ought not to be talking to you about it,' she said presently. 'My work's such that I'm not permitted to discuss—er—things with anyone, but I'm so troubled about you. I was intending to send a letter by the supply boat because I felt——'

'Alma,' broke in Reyna urgently, 'what are you trying to say to me?'

'Thor Granville's had the deeds altered——' Again Alma stopped, this time as if she already regretted having voiced the startling piece of information. She looked pained, and yet angry at the same time. 'He's made it look as if all that you own is a small acreage called Orchid Bay, at the very southern tip of the island—in fact, as far away as possible from the site of his new house.'

All this time Reyna could only stare in disbelief. To have deeds altered? Surely that was not possible! And if it was possible, then the new deeds were quite obviously a forgery.

'Are you sure, Alma?' she managed at last. 'He—he can't—I mean, he wouldn't—oh, no, you must be mistaken! Thor wouldn't do such a thing to me!'

'He would and he has!' Anger had now taken over from the hesitancy which Alma had shown before. She was determined to tell Reyna everything. 'A friend of his, a Mr Gieves who works for him, did the alteration——'

'Richard Gieves? But how can he? Is he a qualified person in such things?'

Alma nodded her head.

'Fred knows him—at least, he knows of him. He was a land surveyor working with one of London's biggest estate agents until about a year ago. There was some scandal—he fell in love with the wife of one of the partners and decided to leave England rather than break up the marriage. Thor Granville was his friend from university days and

Richard wrote to him explaining what had happened. Mr Granville offered him a job in one of his hotels on Beau Vallon Beach. But he must have asked this Richard Gieves to do this job for him—the alteration to the deeds, that is. Fred told me all this because, when I saw these new deeds, I was naturally so perturbed that I just had to tell my brother. He's baffled by the whole thing. Mr Granville's well thought of on Mahé and Fred just couldn't believe that he'd stoop to anything so infamous, but he has,' she ended, spreading her hands in a gesture of anger.

Reyna shook her head.

'I still can't believe it,' she said, yet her thoughts had switched to that dinner, when she had met Richard and sensed the guilty feeling he had each time he looked at her. 'You say that in these new deeds all I have is Orchid Bay?'

'That's right. Do you know it?'

'Yes; it's a very pretty little bay, very pretty indeed.'

'Well, according to these new deeds it's yours—and you have nothing else.'

'My little house——' Reyna began.

'Is his, according to this document.'

'He can't do it!' cried Reyna, anger now replacing the pain of Thor's dastardly act. 'How does he think he can get away with it?'

'I don't know, but, to my surprise, Fred seems to think he can. It would appear that the island never was well-defined as regards its boundaries.'

'No,' admitted Reyna, 'it wasn't.' So many things were coming into her mind: the doubts and uncertainties, the strangeness of Celia's attitude when Reyna had ordered her off her land. There was Ouma's assertion that the whole of the island belonged to Thor. 'I'm so confused,' Reyna owned, her voice edged with distress. 'Richard and Thor *were* looking round one day.'

'Making the survey, seeing just how the forgery could be made to look authentic!' Alma looked at the food on her plate as if the very sight of it choked her. 'I was so furious when Fred said that Mr Granville would probably get away with it. I couldn't help thinking of your little Creole villa, and all the work you'd put into it! To have it taken from you is just not on!'

'I shall fight him,' asserted Reyna, but instantly her eyes became dulled. 'I can't; I haven't any money to fight him in court.'

'You could make some inquiries while you're here today. I know of a good solicitor, and if we rang him he might be able to see you. Does that course appeal to you?'

'Yes . . .' But what about the expense? She had practically spent everything she came out with. 'Could I send him his fee when I return to England, do you think?'

'I should say yes. He's a very understanding man, and he knows me. I'll willingly vouch for you.'

'That's kind of you, Alma.' But Reyna hesitated, feeling sure that the visit to the solicitor would not prove of much benefit to her. 'Perhaps I'd better wait,' she said apologetically. 'I'll take advice when I get back to England.'

'Are you sure?' Alma was clearly very upset. 'If there was only something I could do——'

'You've done a lot already, by warning me of what's going on. When I get back I'll see the solicitors who did everything after Patch—Mr Harper—died.'

'The previous owner? Fred was saying that Mr Granville was furious with the old man, trying to force him to sell his half of the island.'

'That's quite true.'

'I wonder why Mr Granville didn't have the deeds altered before?' mused Alma.

'He believed he'd get the whole of the island very soon anyway, because Mr Harper was ninety-seven. He'd left his half to charity and Mr Granville assumed he'd be able to buy it for a lot less than it was worth, once Mr Harper had died, that was.'

'He sounds a thoroughly detestable character!'

Reyna's mouth quivered. The proof was there, yet she hated the idea of Thor's intention of robbing her. She felt sure that he would not have had the deeds altered unless he was confident of getting away with it. Illegal it must be, but with the utter confusion over the demarcation line which divided the island, he had been able to institute the forgery.

Alma was looking at her watch, a worried frown upon her brow.

'I'm afraid I must leave you,' she said reluctantly.

'That's all right, Alma.'

'We must keep in touch.'

'I was intending to invite you over to my villa, but now——' Reyna broke off, swallowing the little lump that had risen in her throat. Was all the work she had put in to come to nothing?

'You have my address, and you can always ring me at the office.' Alma rose urgently. 'I'm sorry to be rushing off, but the boss isn't the understanding type, worse luck!'

Reyna left the café less than five minutes after her friend. She wandered about the town for a while, bewildered and so unhappy that she could have wept. There was so much she did not understand, since even now she was having great difficulty in accepting the fact that Thor was intending to rob her. Yet Alma had given her proof that this was so. Why had not Thor taken the whole of her half, though? Why should he have left her one of the most beautiful bays on the island? From the first he had wanted the *whole* of Surcoufe, had spoken with complete confidence of getting it. Had he been forced, when having the deeds altered, to leave her a small portion of land? That did not make sense. If he could take some, then surely he could take all.

'But no one can blatantly alter deeds and appropriate someone else's land!' No, it was impossible. A deep sigh

escaped her, for she was right back to the beginning: Thor
Granville *had* altered the deeds, and he *was* appropriating
her land.

Suddenly Reyna was colliding with someone. Firm hands
steadied her and she looked up into the amused eyes of
Richard Gieves.

'You!' she exclaimed, snatching herself away from his
hold. 'Keep your hands off me!' All the loathing she felt
for him was in her eyes, and she would have turned and
sped away had he not grasped her wrist.

'What's wrong?' he demanded. 'Anyone would think '
had the plague, or something!'

Reyna swallowed, aware that she had said something
that would be difficult to explain away without revealing
what she knew about those deeds.

'Please,' she said, trying unsuccessfully to snatch her
hand away, 'leave me alone. I'm—I'm very upset.'

'So it would appear.' His glance was strange, almost perceptive. 'Can you tell me what's upset you, Reyna?'

She shook her head, and tugged at her hand again. And
then, to her dismay, she started to cry.

'G-go away!' she said fiercely. 'Go away, I said!'

'And leave you like this? Not likely.' He transferred his
hand to her elbow, steering her towards a seat beneath
some trees. 'Sit down,' he said gently, 'and tell Uncle
Richard what's wrong.'

She looked at him sideways, through her tears. It had
just occurred to her that she could denounce him without
having to mention Alma, since neither he nor Thor had
any idea that they knew each other, so there was no chance
of their making a guess as to where Reyna had received her
information.

'I happen to know that you and Thor have been up to
some villainy over my half of Surcoufe!' There, it was out,
and he could begin thinking about it! 'He's trying to rob
me!'

'I see ...' He had coloured slightly, and he lapsed into a thoughtful silence for a while. 'You believe that new deeds have been produced?'

'I know that new deeds have been produced!'

Richard turned towards her.

'How do you know? Have you been to the Land Registry Office here?' He gave her no time to answer as he went on, 'You must have done, because otherwise you wouldn't have known about the deeds.' He paused. 'At least not yet awhile,' he added as an afterthought.

'Aren't you ashamed of yourself?' His calmness perturbed her, filled her with foreboding. 'I noticed, at that dinner we had with Thor, that you looked guilty every time you glanced at me. You'd already promised to change those deeds for Thor.' It was a statement, but Richard was shaking his head.

'It wasn't guilt, Reyna, it was pity. I was sorry for you because you were obviously thrilled with the idea of owning half of such a beautiful island——'

'You were sorry for me,' she flashed, 'but you were still willing to assist Thor in trying to rob me!' Although there was heat in her words she had a sinking feeling in the pit of her stomach. And Richard's long silence did not help; he was frowning, preoccupied, indecisive. But at last he turned towards her again and, looking straightly at her, he said slowly,

'Reyna, this is going to hurt you, but it must be said, no matter if it makes Thor mad. The island of Surcoufe— *the whole of it*—belongs to Thor. He bought it outright from the man whose grandfather had, by some means, come into possession of both halves.'

'Owns ... the whole ... of Surcoufe ...?' Reyna was shaking her head, yet, deep within her, she was accepting Richard's words as the truth. 'But if he owned it all, then why was he willing to buy——' She stopped, shaking her head again. 'It doesn't make sense,' she quivered, bringing out a handkerchief to dry her cheeks.

'Perhaps not, because you don't really know Thor. He's a man of honour, and when he realised that Mr Harper's half of the island had somehow come illegally into another man's possession he was very angry indeed. He bought Surcoufe in all good faith—and in fact the man who sold it to him was honest enough. It was this man's grandfather who had done something shady; he bought the half owned by Julie and Melidor, but a short while later he managed to get his hands on that half owned by Mr Harper. It was trickery of some kind, but it worked, owing to the absurd way the island had been divided in the first place. The whole of the island ended up on one set of deeds. Thor received those deeds when he bought the island a few years ago.'

Reyna sat silent, digesting all this, and at the same time realising that there must be a good deal yet to be told.

'The Mr Harper you referred to was the father of the man —the Mr Harper who left me half of the island?'

'Yes, that's right.'

'And he never knew of this—er—robbery?'

'Seems not. He left his half to his son—the man whom you knew.'

'Patch,' murmured Reyna to herself. 'It's strange that it didn't all come out when Patch's father died.'

'You have to remember that there was nothing legal taking place at that time. This Patch you mention merely took over, never realising that he was not the owner of the half which had been in his family since the days of the pirates. He was obsessed with the idea of a vast treasure and also he really loved the island. So Thor apparently hadn't the heart to turn round and tell him that he'd no right on the island.'

'I still can't understand how the matter of the trickery went unnoticed.'

'The Harpers didn't spend much time on Surcoufe, re-member. Patch's grandfather did live on it for a time—in fact, Patch's father was born on Surcoufe. But there was no work and so it really wasn't possible for anyone to settle there.'

'Julie and Melidor did,' Reyna reminded him.

'They were content to live on what they could produce. They were exceptional,' Richard added, and Reyna had to admit that this was true. 'The man who appropriated Mr Harper's half never lived on Surcoufe at all,' went on Richard. 'In fact, the island's been more uninhabited than habited, as apart from that couple, and the woman who took in all the stray dogs from Mahé, no one has spent much time at all on Surcoufe since its capture by the pirates.'

Reyna nodded. She was marvelling at the way she had resigned herself to the fact that she no longer had any right on Surcoufe. She was aware of a deep sense of loss, which was natural, but alongside this was a certain measure of relief that the mystery that had been troubling her since she set foot on the island was at last being cleared up. However, there was still much that she wanted to know, and she referred to Richard's statement that Thor had not the heart to tell Patch that he did not own half of Sur-coufe.

'He knew that some dirty work had taken place,' ex-plained Richard. 'He was aware that the Harpers had been robbed. So he offered to buy Patch's half——'

'He'd have paid money out twice for the same land?'

'That was his way, Reyna. Mind you, he'd got the island at a very fair price—less than it was worth, he told me, but the man selling it was satisfied and so the deal went through quite amicably. However, Thor felt he ought to recompense Mr Harper—Patch, as we've called him—and so he offered to buy him out. The old man was stubborn and accused Thor of trying to swindle him, asserting that he was preventing people from buying, which he was, of course.' Richard stopped and Reyna continued, telling him that she knew about that.

'Patch believed that Thor was trying to rob him of the treasure,' she went on. 'But I don't believe there is any treasure, do you?'

He shook his head.

'No one does. It's only legend. You always get that where you have islands raided and occupied by pirates. Richard paused, but Reyna was thoughtfully silent and he continued, 'It came as a shock to Thor to find that Patch had left his half to a woman, as Thor had hoped, when the old man died, to prove his ownership and have the matter settled without further difficulty. He told me that he hoped that the lady would understand, once he explained the position. However, he decided to make some inquiries concerning the legatee, and when he found out that she was a young schoolteacher he had the same qualms of conscience that had caused him to be so generous with Patch. The young woman would be so disappointed at receiving a legacy and then discovering it was worth nothing after all that he resignedly accepted the position as it had stood before.'

'Not quite the same,' said Reyna reflectively. 'He expected that the young woman would be only too eager to sell out to him.'

'That's right. He was furious, I must admit, at your obstinacy. His patience had been sorely tried already, as you can imagine, with Patch. He didn't want anyone else on his island, which is not unreasonable, is it?'

'No, indeed it isn't.'

'And so he tried his best to get you to sell out to him.

'He was willing to give me money for nothing.' Despite her dejection at her loss Reyna felt a lightness in her heart that seemed to compensate in full for that loss. Thor, the man she loved, was not a rogue and a thief after all. On the contrary, he was a rather wonderful person who hated to hurt people, so much so that he had been willing to expend a considerable amount of money over and above what he had paid for the island in the first place.

And all she had done was to defy him, to remain loyal to poor old Patch. She had threatened to exploit her half of the island—not that this had upset Thor in any way at all. And no wonder, since he could at any time he chose have ordered her off the island altogether. Richard was speaking again, referring to the altered deeds.

'Thor realised just how much you'd come to love the island, Reyna, and he found he just couldn't turn you off it altogether. And so he asked me to make a new set of deeds, giving you that delightful little bay. I myself felt sorry for you because obviously you believed you owned half the island.'

'But it was most generous of Thor to make me a gift of Orchid Bay.' Reyna was not intending to accept the gift, however. It was unfair to Thor, since he obviously would prefer to have the island all to himself. This thought led to another ... to that moment when she had asked herself if it were possible that he could care for her. She said, looking at Richard,

'Celia ... is she ... I mean ... Are they in love?'

'Thor was engaged to her once, but she let him down— chose another man. But then she changed her mind and broke off this engagement too. I often feel that Thor and she will marry in the end.' So casual. He had no idea why Reyna had put the question. 'I must go,' he said with a hint of apology. 'I came into Victoria to do some urgent shopping. I'm going back now to the hotel where I work.'

'The Cordia,' she said. 'Why did Thor not want you to reveal to me where you worked?'

Richard looked surprised by the question; Reyna explained about the impression she had gained on the night of the dinner party.

'I think it must have been because he was having the

deeds altered. He probably didn't want you to know too much about me, to know that I was capable of altering the deeds.'

'So that I would never connect you with it? But it wouldn't have mattered, would it?'

'Thor wasn't intending that you should know it was a gift,' he explained. 'It was his intention to tell you, as kindly as possible, that it was only a small part of the island that Patch had owned—Orchid Bay and the nice little plot at the back of it.'

'Will Thor be vexed with you, then, for telling me all this?'

'I expect he won't be pleased. But there was nothing else for it, was there—not when I found myself confronted with that accusation?'

'No, I suppose not.' She looked at him gratefully. I'm glad you've told me everything, Richard. I know what to do now.'

'What to do?' He looked alarmed. 'What do you mean?'

'I'm leaving Surcoufe for ever——'

'You can't do that, Reyna. He'll blame himself—no, he'll blame me!'

'What does it matter? He has a right to the whole of the island. I shan't accept his gift. In any case, it isn't any good to me, is it? I've no money to build myself a holiday home at Orchid Bay.' Her voice broke a little, but Richard did not notice. Reyna was thinking of the little Creole villa which she had brought back to life—the villa where Julie and Melidor spent so very many happy years, from youth through maturity and into old age. It would return to what it was when first Reyna had discovered it ...

The return trip to Surcoufe was an ordeal to Reyna, and because she was so quiet Thor himself seemed to become totally lost in thought. She was glad to say goodnight to him and to make her way from the cabin, where he had left her, to the villa. But the pleasure and feeling of excitement that always assailed her on entering the house was no longer there; she stood on the threshold and the tears fell unrestrainedly down her face. So many hours of pleasure, so much hard work, but done willingly in expectation of the reward. She had visualised the future, when with all her savings going into the house, she would produce something she could really be proud of. And now it was just a dream from which she had been awakened . . .

She closed the door and lit the lamp; its mellow glow spread a lovely warmth around the room and on to the polished wooden walls. Suddenly she felt she could not stay on the island even for the days left to her. The supply boat would come tomorrow; she would be on it.

But there was so much to pack. If she did not begin tonight she would never get the boat in the morning. She found herself weeping at the thought of all she would have to leave behind. Impossible to take the furniture, for one thing, or her kitchen utensils, her rugs and curtains and cushions.

Determinedly she put all this from her and, going into the bedroom, she took out one of her suitcases and began to pack it. So absorbed was she in this task that she had no idea that Thor had entered the living-room, and was now standing in the doorway, his astonished gaze fixed on her bent figure.

'Reyna—what on earth——?'

'Thor!' She stared at him from her side of the bed. 'How —how d-did you get in? I didn't—didn't bolt the door, I think?'

He spread his hands, glancing all around.

'When did you do all this? How did you get it so well fixed up?'

The tears fell abundantly now, blinding her.

'It doesn't matter. I know the truth. I'm leaving tomorrow, so I've to pack. Will you please see that Ouma gets all—all th-these th-things ...?' A sob choked the rest and for a long moment there was silence in the room.

'Seaching for the treasure ... was what you said ...' Thor's voice was so quiet that she hardly caught the words. 'I ought to have suspected something ... and yet why should I? This place was—or appeared to be—a total wreck when I last saw it, so obviously I wouldn't think of your doing it up.' He glanced around as he spoke, his voice still no more than a murmur revealing his thoughts. 'What a delightful little place it is.' His eyes came at length to rest on Reyna's tear-stained face. 'How did you manage it?' he asked again, ignoring the little plaintive whimper coming from outside where Shah was sitting by the front door.

Reyna found herself talking, explaining, the words tumbling out often in disjointed sentences. But she saw by his expression that Thor understood, that he was taking everything in, from the moment when she discovered the little Creole house, forlorn and forgotten, to the moment when she had learned from Richard that the whole of the island belonged to Thor.

'It was kind of you to make me a gift of—of Orchid Bay,' she continued, with now and then a tiny sob catching her voice. 'But I can't accept it. I w-wanted—wanted th-this little house. I d-did it up for myself, of c-course, but for Julie and Melidor as well, because—because they h-had been so happy here——' She looked at him across the room. 'I know they were happy, because it's got that sort of atmosphere——' Again she broke off, to brush the tears from her cheeks. 'Please go,' she begged. 'I've a lot to do if I'm to catch the supply boat tomorrow.'

Thor, making no effort to do as she asked, stood where he was, one hand resting on the polished jamb of the door.

'You haven't asked me how I come to be here,' he said.

'You must have seen the light. Didn't you go home after you left me at the door of the cabin?'

'I turned back. I wanted to say something to you.'

'About the island? You were going to explain about Orchid Bay?' Reyna had no idea why she should be saying this. All she did know was that she wanted him to leave, so that she could get on with the task of packing all those things which she hoped to take with her. 'I've made up my mind. I won't accept the gift. It wouldn't be fair to take advantage of your generosity, and of the fact that you're sorry for me.' Automatically she brushed a hand across her cheek again, while with the other hand she picked up some underwear from a drawer and dropped it into the suitcase. 'No, it wouldn't be fair; you don't want intruders on your island.'

'No, I certainly don't want intruders on my island.'

'So I must go——'

'You still haven't asked me how I come to be here.'

'You saw the light,' she said again. 'You were bound to discover my activities one day. I've known that all along.'

'I'm here, Reyna, because I've something to say to you.' Thor took a couple of strides that brought him close to the bed.

'Yes—well, you've said it, and I've told you I won't accept your gift.'

'I'm not aware that the gift has even been mentioned by me.'

'Thor,' she pleaded, 'please go. If I'm to catch that boat in the morning I must do my packing—or some of it— tonight.'

'What,' inquired Thor from the other side of the bed, 'makes you think you'll be catching the supply boat in the morning?'

'I can't stay—I won't ...' Reyna's voice drifted away to a breathless silence as she saw, through a mist of tears, the expression in Thor's eyes. 'I m-must go ... m-mustn't I?' she added, in so absurd a manner that Thor could scarcely suppress laughter. But he did suppress it, feeling that this was not exactly the right moment to bring mirth into the situation. Instead, he moved to her side of the bed, to stand for a moment looking down at her with the kind of expression that made her heart turn right over, quickening her pulse, tightening her muscles so that she could not have moved even if she wanted to. His hand came from his side to take hold of hers. She was gripping a silk headscarf which she had taken from a drawer; Thor unloosed it and dropped it lightly on to the bed. He said, tilting her chin with his hand,

'There seems to be a great deal of explaining to be done by both of us, but I think we shall take everything in order of priority.' The hint of a pause and then, 'Will you marry me, my love?'

She stared, her mind registering the fact that she had more than once speculated on the possibility of his caring for her.

'I d-don't know wh-what to say——' Her stammering words were cut as Thor drew her gently into his arms.

'I'm very sure you do, my darling. You see, I happen to know that you're just as much in love with me as I am with you.'

'So—so you did guess,' she said simply. 'Celia assured me that you——' She broke off, but not quickly enough. Thor held her from him, and he was frowning, she noticed. He opened his mouth to say something born of anger, but changed his mind and said, bringing her to him again,

'Yes, my dearest, I did guess—it wasn't so difficult, you know,' he added tenderly, looking into her eyes and reading in them all that his heart could desire. 'You gave yourself away . . . by looking at me as you're looking at me now——'

'Oh, no! I'm sure I didn't——!'

'My love, don't argue with me. I must warn you, right at the start, that I shall be a tyrant to live with!'

'I'll—I'll take a chance on—on it,' she returned huskily.

'I have a confession to make regarding my guess that you loved me, but, as I just said, first things first——' The next moment Reyna's heart seemed to be throbbing to suffocation as, her slender body crushed against the unrelenting strength of his, she knew the rapture of his kiss, tender yet possessive, reverent and yet masterfully demanding as Thor's lips took their fill, holding hers in captivity until, gasping for breath, she pleaded for release by pressing her hand against his chest.

'Thor, I can't—can't——' She stopped to take in a draught of air. 'I can't believe it! Only a few minutes ago I was so unhappy, thinking I'd have to leave all this.' She leaned away to spread a hand. 'You said it was delightful. I'm so very glad you like it, Thor. I hoped you would.'

'It's enchanting. You're a real home-maker, my love.' He paused for a moment, as if not too happy about what he was going to say. But presently he did begin to talk, and Reyna learned that, having guessed that she was in love with him, Thor had brought Celia over, so that Reyna would think he had someone else.

'As at that time I had no intention of giving up my freedom,' he continued ruefully, 'I felt it only fair to put you off, as it were. At that dinner I intended to put on an act with Celia—a lover-like act—in order to cure you, but when I saw you standing there, looking so beautiful and so desirable in that dress you'd bought from Ouma, I instantly regretted having brought Celia over to Surcoufe. He stopped a moment. 'When you were talking to Celia, did she tell you we were once engaged?'

'She said you'd known one another for years,' was all Reyna answered in reply to that, at which Thor went on to tell all that Richard had already told her. She listened, filling in any gaps he left with what she had overheard when he and Celia were talking together after he had brought the girl over. When he had finished speaking Reyna asked if Celia knew that he owned the whole of the island.

'Yes, she did.' Thor looked down into Reyna's face, a

hint of amusement in his eyes. 'You ordered her off your land, she told me.'

Reyna bit her lip, but Thor, understanding her embarrassment, bent and kissed her, on her mouth, her throat, her hair.

'I've been so blind, Thor,' Reyna admitted when presently he drew away from her. 'There were so many signs; I should have guessed that you owned the whole island.'

'No, I can't agree. Old Harper truly believed he owned half, so naturally he'd sound convincing to you.'

'But I had so many misgivings, Thor.'

'Yes, I'll agree there,' he said. 'You must have been very bewildered by my attitude, especially when you came along with all those threats about development,' he added with a humorous smile.

'You knew I was poor!' she accused, her lovely eyes darkening with indignation. 'It was horrid of you to play a game with me like that!'

'You deserved it!'

She thought about that and agreed that she had deserved it.

'But Patch had said so much about your—er—roguery...'

'And a lot more. Come on, out with it! What else did he have to say about me?'

Reyna told him and he laughed heartily.

'The poor old chap. I feel I ought to have had more patience with him.'

'That's not fair to yourself. You were wonderful, Thor, refraining from telling him the truth, that he didn't own any part of this island. And it was incredibly generous of you to offer to buy half an island that you already owned anyway.'

Thor passed that off, going on to explain how he had taken Richard over the island so that the new deeds could be brought into being.

'It was all something of a muddle in my mind,' he went on to admit, 'since even then I'd begun to think that there was to be no escape for me.

Reyna had to laugh.

'And so there was really no necessity for you to give me Orchid Bay?'

'No need at all,' he owned, catching some of her laughter.

She told him about Alma, and how at first she had believed that he was taking land from her rather than giving it to her.

'I felt terrible,' she ended, and at the catch in her voice Thor realised just how much she was hurt by her discovery.

'Well, it's all explained now, my dearest.' Thor drew her close, tilting her face to kiss her. 'I suppose I ought to have capitulated sooner,' he owned ruefully. 'But after my affair with Celia I'd sworn never to become involved with a woman again. Life seemed so much smoother without them, so totally without complications.' He paused and smiled, and brushed the softly-parted lips with his own. 'I was troubled about you in that cabin but hoped you'd be so uncomfortable that you'd leave the island and never want to return. Then, later, I was even more concerned after I'd half-admitted to myself that I was falling in love with you. I wanted to have you at the villa with me, but after that night when we were both tempted I knew I dared not offer you a spare bedroom at the Villa Surcoufe. His eyes twinkled in the most attractive way. 'I couldn't have resisted you any more than you could have resisted me, my dearest.'

She coloured, naturally, but was honest enough not to argue with what he had said. For she had come as close to succumbing to temptation that night as ever it was possible to do. Her thoughts switched to this particular evening, and the journey back from Victoria to Surcoufe. Thor had been silent, but only because she herself was silent. She said, just because she had to,

'What made you come tonight, Thor? I mean, you didn't seem, on the boat, to—to be in love with me.'

He frowned at her and shook his head.

'You were so far away from me,' he answered. 'I can see now that you would be quiet, having learned that you didn't own any of Surcoufe and that you believed you would be leaving all this. But as for me—well, I felt I couldn't get near to you at all, and for one rather grim period I wondered if I'd been mistaken in thinking that you loved me. However, once I'd left you at the cabin and began to walk back home, I knew I wouldn't rest until I'd talked to you. I also knew that I hadn't been mistaken in thinking that you loved me, so I turned around and went back to the cabin. You can imagine what I felt like when you weren't there. I called several times, thinking that you might have decided to take a stroll along the beach. Obviously you didn't hear me, and so I started along the beach myself, and then I saw the light in the distance, through the trees. Just what I expected I couldn't have said—certainly not this——' He broke off, shaking his head. 'How you managed it alone is quite incredible!'

'It was such fun, Thor,' she told him enthusiastically. 'To make something live again——! And wait until you see what I've done outside! Did you notice the nameplate, by the way?'

'No, I didn't.'

She looked a little disappointed, and Thor, taking her by the hand, moved over to the door which separated the bedroom from the living-room.

'Come and show me,' he invited, and together they went out into the starlit night. He had his torch and he snapped it on as they took the narrow little path, Shah at Thor's heels.

'There!' Reyna pointed and Thor shone the light on to the wooden sign. 'I did it all myself!'

'Villa Samana,' he said softly. 'Charming.'

'There's a samana tree at the bottom of the garden——' Reyna swung a hand. 'Over there, in the side garden but at the end.'

'What a pleasant time you must have had.' Thor glanced down at her, his eyes filled with tender admiration. 'You're a very clever girl. We must keep the Villa Samana like this always.'

'Can we?' She looked doubtful. 'What can we use it for?'

'We'll think of something——' He broke off, his lips curving in amusement. 'The children could have it for a Wendy house,' he suggested.

Reyna thought that nothing could be nicer than to have children playing in the little Creole villa.

'I'd like that,' she said, and felt Thor's fingers tighten lovingly around hers before he brought her hand to his lips and kissed it.

'Darling, I know it's very late, but I'm wide awake. Shall we stroll on the beach for a while?'

'I'd love to!' she answered, eagerly, impulsively, without stopping to think that her heightened emotions could spell danger, or to remember that other evening when peril had certainly hovered very close indeed. Thor pulled her to him, his arm about her waist. Reyna rested her head against his shoulder and they walked in silence along the path that led to the palm-fringed beach. All was so quiet beneath the star-spangled sky, a deep purple sky, vast and mysterious, its colour intense. On the beach the palms and casuarinas sighed as the zephyr of a breeze caressed their foliage—and then there was silence again. Reyna, caught in a magic spell of sublime enchantment, glanced up at her lover in wonderment, marvelling that she should be here at all. If Janie had not recommended that inn; if Patch had not appeared at that particular time; if she had refused to accept his gift ... 'And if you, my love, had not been living here——' She stopped abruptly, blushing at the realisation that she had whispered this last few words aloud. Thor stopped, looking down into her lovely face, a question in his eyes.

A shaky, selfconscious little laugh fell on the silent air.

'I was thinking of all the "ifs" that changed my life. You see, I haven't told you how I came to meet Patch. And I never would have met him if one of my colleagues hadn't mentioned the Mermaid Inn at Rye ...' Reyna went on to relate all that had happened, laughing now and then at Thor's changing expression. 'It's quite a story, isn't it?' she ended, twisting a little, so that she faced him.

'Quite a story,' he agreed. 'The cantankerous old scamp!'

'Aren't you glad that he decided to do something absurd, and give me half of the island?'

'You know darned well I'm glad!' Thor took her to him, tilting her face and gazing down into it for a long, long while before, bending his head, he kissed her soft, inviting lips. Eagerly she responded, thrilling to the hard mastery of his body so close to hers, to the tender touch of a hand on the curve of her breast, to the sheer bliss and magic that surrounded her—the warm tropical island, the shimmering diamonds tumbling over the reef, the drowsy lagoon, lambent beneath the gentle play of moonglow. She sighed, and nestled her head against his shoulder.

'And to think,' she murmured, almost sleepily, 'that I didn't believe in the treasure.'

'Nor did I. Yet we've found one, haven't we, my darling?'

She nodded, raising her head.

'The treasure of love,' she whispered. 'A treasure above all others.'

Poignant tales of love, conflict, romance and adventure

Harlequin Presents...

Elegant and sophisticated novels of
great romantic fiction . . .
12 All time best sellers.

Join the millions of avid Harlequin readers all
over the world who delight in the magic of a
really exciting novel.

**From the library of Harlequin Presents all time best sellers —
we are proud and pleased to make available the 12 selection
listed here.**

Combining all the essential elements you expect of great
story telling, and bringing together your very favourite
authors — you'll thrill to these exciting tales of love, conflict,
romance, sophistication and adventure. You become involve
with characters who are interesting, vibrant, and alive. Their
individual conflicts, struggles, needs, and desires, grip you,
the reader, until the final page.

Have you missed any of these *Harlequin Presents...*

Offered to you in the sequence in which they were originally printed — this is an opportunity for you to add to your Harlequin Presents . . . library.

This elegant and sophisticated series was first introduced in 1973, and has been a huge success ever since. The world's top romantic fiction authors combine glamour, exotic locales, dramatic and poignant love themes woven into gripping and absorbing plots to create an unique reading experience in each novel.

You'd expect to pay $1.75 or more for this calibre of best selling novel, — at only **$1.25 each**, Harlequin Presents are truly top value, top quality entertainment.

Don't delay — order yours today

Complete and mail this coupon today!